A Turbulent Road to Heaven

ISBN – 13: 978-1482746457

ISBN – 10: 148274645X

Visit Dr. Luke A.M. Brown & Mrs. Berthalicia
Fonseca-Brown's at
www.ShopforBigDeals.com/heavenlydeals,

This is a work of fiction. Names, characters, places, and
incidents are either the product of the author's
imagination or are used fictitiously, and any resemblance
to actual persons, living or dead, business
establishments, events or locales is, coincidental.

A Turbulent Road to Heaven

Dr. Luke A. M. Brown
Mrs. Berthalicia Fonseca-Brown

DEDICATION

Mrs. Estelle Streete Brown –

For our late mother, Mrs. Estelle Streete Brown. We love you.

Genève Williams –

 We are thankful to Geneve Williams, to whom we owe all our success.

Myrettle Williams –

For our late sister, Myrette Williams. We love you.

THANK YOU

We also dedicate this book to our late sister, Beverly Allen, and late nephew, Caple Allen-Browdie.

We thank our cousin, Junior, for being a supportive fan.

Prologue

He paused for a moment. He looked at the audience in the small district church and shot a quick glance at his brothers, Karl and Bunny, in the front row. He thought about his other brother, Junior, who was unable to make the trip to Jamaica for the funeral. He continued, "The honorable heroine, Essie Brown, also known to her hometown folks as Miss Pretty, was born on March 26, 1922 near Cascade, a small town in Hanover."

Dr. Leonard shuffled his papers in his hands as he scrambled to find the correct page to read.

His nerves got the better of him for a moment, but he gathered himself and continued reading. "At nine months of age, she was brought to Cascade to live with her new parents, Mum and Amos. She later moved to Montego Bay to live with her friend, Nurse Ferguson. As a teenager, the brave Essie moved out on her own."

He cleared his throat and projected his voice so he could be heard by the congregation members mumbling in the back of the church. "She bore eight children, four boys and four girls, Gena, Junior, Betty, Lela, Myrtle, Karl, me, and Bunny.

"She was blessed with more than twenty-six grandchildren, of which the two youngest were Alexander M. Brown and Algivanni G. Brown. She had more than twenty-one great-grandchildren. She loved and cherished each grandchild.

She said that children were blessings sent from God. She was also blessed with a host of nieces, nephews, cousins, friends, and extended family members."

Dr. Leonard paused, adjusted his collar, and continued his emotional but detailed eulogy with an undertone of rage and exigency. It was as if he was mad at the world and wanted everyone to know who Essie was. Like a lieutenant, he paused and braced himself for his next statement. In a loud voice, Dr Leonard said, "Today, for what it's worth, I bestow the honor of heroism on Mrs. Essie Brown for the long, hard battle that she fought in her life. She fought to give her family a better life and to make this earth a better place. A hero is an unselfish person who risks his or her life to save another. Well, my mother did that. As a shy, vulnerable country girl, she came to town to make a living. Instead, she ended up dedicating her life to her family, giving up everything else so that her family could have a brighter future."

He shot another glance at his grieving family in assorted black apparel in the left front row of the Glenworth church. He gazed at his handwritten notes, before continuing with the same enthusiasm. "Success was not easy. She struggled to play the role of both mother and father to her children, and as if that was not enough, she cared for many other kids along the way. Many times, she would go into town to shop and would see a young lady in the streets with nowhere to go, and she would not hesitate to take that young lady home to join her already-too-large family. This kind virtue she has done many times in her life." He held his head up and glanced at Pauline sitting in the front row with his family all dressed in black. He continued, "Today, one or two of these ladies might be amongst us in this church because of her kind virtues."

Dr. Leonard switched to a softer tone, but nonetheless, he was still eager to let the congregation know the caliber of human being that this world had lost. "By this time, she had learned to put her troubles behind her with a little whisper of prayer. She struggled in life, but she gave her absolute all to her family. Essie was a true fighter in the forefront of the army when there was a battle to be won for her family."

As Essie's second youngest child, Dr. Leonard Brown lost no passion as he continued the eulogy at his mother's funeral. "The biggest turning point in my mother's life came at the age of fifty-four. This was when she found God. She found herself through her religion. She also got married on April 11, 1976 to Timothy Brown."

Dr. Leonard insisted that this was the moment to celebrate and praise Essie's virtuous life. This was his last shot to let the world know that his mother was a woman of substance. He had much to say and little time to do so. He was overflowing with guilt. He knew that he had failed in his promise to his mother to write a book about her life before she passed away. That day, a detailed eulogy was the best he could do for her, and he was failing at that as well. The world needed to know about her life, but he would have to settle for this small district church audience. Therefore, this was not the time to break down.

Dr. Leonard began closing his eulogy with sadness in his tone, but with the same passion with which he had started. "She went to a better place at 1:00 AM on April 17, 2001. She has gone to a place where there is no more pain, nor sorrow. She is gone to a place where she won't have to fight as hard as she did in this life. She has left us the legacy of hope; if you fight very hard for what you want, you will succeed by all means."

Chapter 1

Bunny was only six years old, but he could sense that being the youngest in Essie's large family was a true attention getter. He had a multitude of brothers and sisters, or so it seemed, to look up to and who, in turn, looked out for his best interests. He had an avalanche of sibling love showering down on him and he was poised to take it all in for what it was worth. He felt special to be Essie's "wash-belly" and even at six, he knew how to capitalize on the benefits of being the youngest of eight kids.

At this point, Leonard was a firm Christian. He taught himself to play the guitar after his sister Gena sent him a toy guitar from the United States. He used it to comfort himself when he was moody or sad. He became sad when he thought of the odds of making it out of his living situation, which were slim. He wanted to be a physician when he grew up, but his family was too poor to consider it with seriousness.

He didn't know the details of what it took to be a physician, but he knew he wanted to be one. His chances of becoming a physician were as good as a Haitian refugee that was heading off to the Miami shores using only a lifeboat, a broomstick, two paddles, and swimming gear to cross the water.

He often thought of the lyrics from one of his favorite songs, sung by Jimmy Cliff: There are "many rivers to cross but I can't seem to find my way over...and it's my will that keeps me alive...and I merely survive because of my pride."

The lyrics of another Jimmy Cliff song helped motivate him: "You can get it if you really want, but you must try, try, and try, try, and try; you'll succeed at last." He made a vow to himself at age ten that he would be a physician or nothing at all.

He also promised Essie that he would one day write a book about her life, so the world would know her true life story. Leonard was young, but he could remember pieces of some of the disasters that had happened in the earlier years with his family.

One particular flashback that he had was of him being in the back of a pickup truck. He was sitting in a compromising position on a pile of furniture. They were on an obscure journey. No one seemed really to know where they were heading. He figured no one knew because everyone in the truck appeared flustered and discomposed. They cried and reassured each other that they would find a place to stay.

He asked few questions about that incident and get even fewer answers, but each time he had that flashback, he thought of ambitiously writing the full story of his mother's life. *Maybe,* he thought to himself, *I'll name that book,* Essie, *as a shortened form of my mother's real name, Estelle.*

Essie loved to hear about Leonard's dreams. She was the only one who took him seriously. She also knew that her life was noteworthy, to say the least. Therefore, she prayed that Leonard's dream would come true one day.

She always hoped that at least one of the seeds she had planted on this earth would grow to become an become an influential figure in this world. When times were unbearably hard, during her pregnancies, these were some of the thoughts that helped her make it through.

It was, therefore, easy for him to convince her to send him to an SDA private high school. Essie did not have the money to pay for the tuition, but she knew it was necessary to try. She signed him up at Harrison Memorial High School. She struggled with the associated costs, but she did everything she could to meet his tuition each semester. Sometimes, she had to borrow money from her neighbors to meet his school expenses.

Leonard, like Myrtle at one time, was now was the only one in his family who was a regular church attendee; Myrtle had dropped out of church. One day, Leonard invited his mother to a crusade meeting that his church was conducting. Essie went with him to that church service. At the end of the service, the minister requested those who might need him to pray for them to come forward to the altar.

Essie reflected on what the minister had said in his ceremony. "God knows that we are only human, and in a lifetime of temptations, we are bound to sin. That is why He sent His son, Jesus. Jesus died for us all so that all our sins may be forgiven. If you accept Christ in your heart, all your sins will be forgiven."

The last phrase was repeated in Essie's mind: "All your sins will be forgiven." Essie surprisingly went to the altar for the minister to pray for her. After the minister finished praying, she was in tears.

For the first time in her life, it dawned on her that Jesus was the only man she needed. If she had Jesus in her life, everything else would fall in line in the right manner. Essie had found salvation. She fell to the ground begging for mercy and forgiveness. She woke up to a brand-new life of Christianity.

Essie left the church that night a changed person. She told Leonard that she was going to quit smoking and drinking that night. She told him that she was going to give her heart to the Lord. Essie's words were simple, but they were bafflingly true. Essie went cold turkey. She never smoked another cigarette. She never took another sip of alcohol. She got baptized within two months of that night after she found God.

Chapter 2

At fourteen, Essie was a strikingly beautiful young woman. She had a humble appearance that allowed her to wear a subtle, pleasant expression wherever she went. She had a small, straight nose which defined her unique profile. She had a small but noticeable mole close to the left side of her upper lip. It complimented her bright, brown eyes-- wise eyes that appeared to be hazel at times, changing color with the tropical sunshine. Her skin was as cool as the fresh, twirling, country breeze in the early morning.

Essie also had glittering black hair that flowed down to the center of her back. She was like a Jamaican mermaid on this tropical island. In the small country town of Cascade where she grew up, it was a rarity to see females with such long, resplendent hair. It was at a time when most young girls put their hair in a single ponytail because their hair was significantly challenged both in length and texture.

Adding to her unusual beauty, Essie had a light complexion. If you saw her once, you would remember her striking beauty. Essie realized at a young age that she stood out in Cascade. There was no other girl like her. Everywhere she went, she was the unsubtle subject.

Essie had a shy, childish smile, but when she laughed, she lost the symmetric lines of her face to happy ones as she lit up with glee. One could detect her happiness from a mile away. When she laughed, it was hard and loud. She loved a good joke and would remain laughing long after everyone else had stopped.

However, Essie was not talkative. She was a very humble, thoughtful, and polite child. It was easy for her to make friends, although she enjoyed being alone. Sometimes she would sit in her huge backyard and stare out over the serene, variegated, green mountain tops deep in thoughts, lost in her own world, like Alice in Wonderland.

She often wondered about her biological mother and why God took her away from her so early in life. Even a black-and-white photo would be consoling to her, if only there was one around.

Essie inherited her beauty from her mother, Doris Lynn. She had a perfect mixture of ethnicities showing Indian, Chinese, and Jamaican features. This explained Essie's long, straight hair and other unique features.

Doris Lynn had just turned eighteen years of age when she got pregnant with Essie. Essie's father was always a mystery. Doris never told anyone how she got pregnant, nor did she name her baby's father. When asked about it, she would change the subject. If she was pushed too hard to discuss it, she would not speak at all. She would shut down all interactions. Sometimes she did not speak to anyone for weeks. Nevertheless, everyone in her family supported her pregnancy. After all, she was of grown age and did not need anyone's consent to start her own family.

Her family was patient with her. They all hoped that after she delivered the baby, she would be less emotional and would open up communication on that oh-so-critical paternal topic.

On the rainy eve of March 26, 1922, shocking news came from the hospital to Doris's family. Doris' mother was frozen at first when she heard the bad news. She stood still, as if afraid any movement would cause her to shatter. She was as still as if she was wrapped tightly in a sheet of wine glasses that were stacked side by side and from head to toe. The only part of her that still moved was her heart, and even her heart was totally out of sync, like a grandfather clock left in an empty house chiming loud and clear, but off rhythm.

Doris had died while giving birth to Essie. No one knew all the details of her death or what exactly had happened. Heartbroken and distraught, the family mourned and wept the loss of their loved one. For many months, long after Doris' funeral, they were depressed and left with many unanswered questions.

Chapter 3

"Essie, wake up. Momma said that you need to clean the house today."

"Rachael, what time is it?" Essie mumbled as she vigorously rubbed her sleepy eyes.

"Time fi get up yuh red dundus pickny, (*time to get up you red speckled colored child*,)" Rachael said to her stepsister in a Jamaican patois dialect. It was 6 a.m. on a Sunday when Rachael went to Essie's room because she(Rachael) was having difficulty sleeping.

"Really Rachael, what time is it? It seems much too early to wake up."

"It is time to get up, you lazy scoundrel," Rachael said with a mean expression on her face.

"What time is it? I'll clean the house. I do it all the time. I just want to know what time it is," Essie said as she insisted on finding out the time from Rachael.

"Lazy pork head, if you want to know the time, why don't you go find out for yourself?" Rachael said rudely.

Groggy and sleepy, Essie crawled out of bed and poked her head into the living room, stealing a peek at the loud, ticking, bright orange clock on the wall. Her hair stood out from her head in disarray, which was blocking her view. She wiped a tendril of hair from her face so she could see the time more clearly. Did it show 6:05 in the morning?

Essie could not believe that Rachael, who should have been sleeping, was up and awake in her room, forcing her to get up to clean the house. Essie rubbed her eyes again in disbelief. It didn't make sense. She curiously peeked through the window to see how it was outside. In clear view, with the aid of the disappearing moonlight, was the old, rusty washbasin that was once white in color but now brown and half buried in the ground like a shallow grave. It was the old familiar landmark of the Streete family's make-believe property boundary on the right side of the house.

It was still dark, but with a misty appearance, a foretaste of the approaching dawn. It was too early to clean the house, especially on a Sunday morning. Everyone was still asleep, except Rachael. Essie knew that she couldn't start cleaning the house even if she wanted to honor Rachael's wish. It would awaken the rest of the Streete family. Then, she would really be in trouble.

Essie went back to her room and saw Rachael standing at her bedroom door with an empty bucket hanging from her left hand. She wondered what dirty trick was she up to.

"Rachael, it's only a little after six. Why are you up so early? Can't sleep?"

"No, I woke up so I have to make sure that you are awake also. You've been living with our family for free.

Life is too easy for you. If I'm up, then you must also be up. Get used to it, you orphan scoundrel."

"Rachael, why don't you go back to bed and try to get some sleep? Count sheep if you have

13

to. When you get up early, what good does that do you?"

"Makes me feel much better, pig face."

Essie thought to herself, *Pig face? Me? She's talking about herself. If our faces were compared side by side, whose face would most likely resemble a pig?*

She dared not breathe a word of such terrible truth.

"Okay, I'm going back to bed Cinderella," Essie said sarcastically to Rachael and made her way back to bed.

"Have a nice dream, pig face," Rachael said, barely stepping aside enough to let Essie squeeze through. Rachael then stood at the door with an evil grin on her face waiting to see Essie's next reaction.

"Oh my God. My bed is soaked! Rachael, what did you do? Did you pour this water onto my bed? You have gone too far now. This is not funny. I'm going to tell Aunt Rose as soon as she wakes up."

"I'll tell momma that you did it. You got angry with me and you wet your bed. Prepare for a beating from dad. As I said, have a nice dream," Rachael chuckled as she left for bed. Essie knew she was right. Aunt Rose would call Uncle Amos to straighten things out. It would no doubt end with an unfair flogging that she could certainly do without. Essie turned her bed onto the other side so that the water could drain. She lay on the floor in disappointment and deep sadness.

* * *

14

Another hungry mouth to feed was the last thing anyone in Doris Lynn's family wanted. It is said that one has to be poor to know the luxury of giving. They felt sorry for their orphan grandchild, but the Lynns had no room or time to raise another child. They already had a large household, and to make matters worse, they were very poor.

Doris' parents, Vera and Danny Lynn, were, small-scale, destitute farmers. Their scope of farming was so small that it seemed as if they farmed solely for themselves. The small piece of nutrient-shy land that comprised their backyard yielded a harvest barely adequate to feed the impoverished family of six in their overcrowded household. Up to the time of Doris' untimely death, Vera and Danny Lynn had four children, not including Doris. They crammed into an old, two-bedroom, country house. The dilapidated house was constructed of mismatched pieces of wood and old rusty sheets of zinc. The sun-drenched, faintly painted house was propped up by four stilts. It crowned the top of the hillside, close to the main road.

In no way were the Lynns willing or able to take on any additional responsibilities. Over their heads with financial burdens, they had nothing left to give.

On the other hand, Rose, Vera's youngest of three sisters, was able to help raise Vera's orphan granddaughter. Aunt Rose had been married to Amos Streete, a skillful handyman and carpenter, for ten years. They had two girls, seven-year-old Rachael and five-year-old Renee. They lived in a modest, four-bedroom house that Amos had built when they first married. Moreover, they had been trying to conceive another child, but had two failed attempts. So, Aunt Rose was more than willing and able to take little baby Essie into their home.

Essie was a pleasant addition to Aunt Rose's family. They were proud of their pretty, newly adopted baby girl. At first, Rachael and Renee were happy to have a new baby sister. They took turns carefully holding and playing with young Essie. She was like a new pet in their home as far as Rachael and Renee were concerned. They called her "pretty" as a nickname. Essie was the perfect addition to their lives.

This blissful union, however, changed as Essie grew older. Essie's adopted sisters grew jealous of her. They acted like the evil stepsisters in *Cinderella*. They did everything in their power to stifle Essie's beauty so they could feel better about themselves. They saw to it that her beauty would not shine through. Unfortunately, the whole Streete family was jealous of Essie. They tried to suppress her confidence any way they could.

Essie tried hard to ignore them, but she often broke down and cried. When the family went to town to shop or have fun, Essie was left alone in the house. She would cry and hope for better days.

Essie most disliked carrying water from the public water pipes. She did it in order to keep the water tanks or reservoirs full at home. It was one of the most demanding tasks she had to do. It was difficult because she had to carry the water in a large bucket back and forth on her head for more than two miles each time.

It seemed unfair that her older sisters rarely had to do this task. When she would complain about it, though, Aunt Rose would shout at her and threaten to call Amos.

This caused her to tremble and shake with a deep fear. Essie knew that Amos' sole contribution would be to administer a flogging. Amos didn't need a reason to beat her. He'd just grab a belt or a stick and start furiously whipping her as hard as he could.

For these reasons and more, Essie dreamed of a better place to live. She knew she had to leave. She didn't know where to go or by what means, but it was just a matter of time. Clearly no longer accepted, she felt that the longer she stayed, the more she strained their welcome.

Chapter 4

Cascade was a rustic, picturesque town, steeped in beauty and located in the Parish of Hanover in the northwestern end of Jamaica. It was a small, quiescent village full of trees, colorful bamboos, a large variety of vegetation, and green valleys, and was encircled by virgin mountain. The town was defined by the village square which lay at the outskirts of the village.

This point was the only means of entering and was the pulse of the tranquil country town. All of the public and private transportation passed through this square on their way to larger cities or towns.

It had a narrow, T-shaped intersection at the town square. At the time, the main public transportation in Cascade consisted of dilapidated, old, overloaded country buses, stuffed with goods and large baskets of freshly harvested farm produce. These ugly shattered old buses would approach the town square from the west in the mornings and return from the east in the evenings, briefly stopping to drop off or pick up passengers at the town square.

It was unusual for any vehicle to use the third leg of the T-shaped road that pointed southward, leading into the inlands of Cascade. The passengers walked to and from these public transports via the third leg of the T- shaped roads. It was interesting to see them get off, fetch their luggage, load it onto their shoulders or heads, and stroll away from the square toward the inlands of Cascade village.

The ones that were leaving the village would have their luggage all jaggedly stacked up on the banking or on the roadside waiting for the bus to arrive. There were a few local shops located at the town square, where most of these travelers would stop. Here they would patronize the shops while they wait for their transportation to arrive.

It was amazing to observe the arrival of these buses. You could hear them from miles away as they blew their horns in warning to indicate that they were close. At this point, everyone who was waiting would gather their luggage and stand at attention as they awaited the approaching bus. All eyes steadfastly focused on the direction of where the vehicle was expected. As the antediluvian vehicle appeared in sight, you could see the piles of loads that were already on top of the bus. It was, at times, so overstocked that the bus would lean to one side as if it were about to fall over.

The most amazing part about these arriving buses was what could be considered as, their equal exchange. Those exiting the bus had about the same amount of containers as those entering the bus. During the heavy activities of loading and unloading, it was difficult to tell who was coming or who was leaving. Everyone was passing some kind of luggage to someone else. After the dust was settled, the previous crowd would have disappeared and the crowd of new arrivals would have been left standing at the village square. They would fetch their load onto their backs, shoulders, or heads and walk away.

The sun-baked road leading into Cascade was paved, but filled with potholes. It was a heart-stirring adventure with breathtaking sceneries on either side of the road as you headed inland. The further inland you went, the more mountainous it became, with scenic hillside landscape and awe-inspiring views of the sea. Even in its antiquity, Cascade was a magnificent land with fresh air and natural beauty to behold.

However, in Essie's opinion, it was not a place to live. In addition to her abusive experiences with her family, Cascade was too small. She dreamed of a time when she could stretch her wings and fly away to be a part of a bigger and better world. Essie dreamed of living in a big city.

Chapter 5

After a five-hour drive through the hills and mountains, fourteen-year-old Essie arrived at Montego Bay, the second largest city and megalopolis of the island of Jamaica. It was the most popular tourist vacation area on the island, a place full of neon lights and white, sandy beaches.

Essie felt that all her life she had been a misplaced piece of a jigsaw puzzle, until that moment. Montego Bay was the right place for her, a place where she belonged. She felt at home. It was a mind-bending, uncanny feeling because, in the midst of an industrious, busy city, with nowhere to go, Essie felt content and right at home.

Essie had worked it out in her head. She would make her way to a busy shopping center and ask a kind-looking lady for a job, one who seemed to need a helping hand, maybe one with kids. She was willing to work for food and shelter. After all, that was basically what she had been doing all her life anyway. She would do anything, whatever it took to survive. Essie realized that her abusive environment back home had been a blessing in disguise; it had prepared her for anything that the big city had to offer or pitch to her. She believed that nothing could be worse than what she had left behind.

After searching the immediate area for a shopping center, she found the perfect place. She boldly walked up to a middle-aged woman and made her best plea. "Good evening miss, my name is Essie from the town of Cascade. I'm here looking for a job, miss. Could you help me? I can do your housekeeping. You don't even have to pay me because I'm willing to work for food and shelter."

"Lard pickni move from in front ta me and go home to yuh parents. What a nice looking child like you doing pon the street? Mi nuh want no liability pon mi self ya mi child," the lady said. "No sir-ree, I don't have no time for foolishness."

Essie realized that people, although they may be decently dressed, were busy, selfish, and self-centered. Some of them would not even stop to listen to her. Either they were overly concerned for her or they treated her with scorn, as if she was a con artist or a person about to rob them of their purses. They seemed to be afraid of her, which she had not expected.

Although Essie knew the big city lifestyle was in her genes, she lost confidence in her plan. Each time she approached another person and was shunned, she felt her belief in those big dreams shrink smaller. It wasn't long before Essie realized that she had not worked everything out properly; indeed, she had no backup plan but to head home. But at six in the evening, it was too late. The last bus back to Cascade left at four.

Essie's excitement turned to panic and fear. The reality of the situation hit her and she was disappointed.

What should I do now? Where am I going to sleep tonight? Panic and fear raced through her empty stomach. She could not hide her fear; it showed in her face.

Essie closed her eyes and breathed a quick word of prayer to God. "Dear heavenly Father, I know that You are up there somewhere watching over everyone. Please guide and protect me this evening. Please, dear Father, show me the way. Send me a good Samaritan, I pray thee. Amen." From the corner of her eyes, Essie noticed a grubby old man watching her from across the street. She walked faster, but the crazy-looking man started following her. He crossed the road to her side and increased his speed. Essie immediately crossed to the other side, but he did the same, closing the distance between them. She started running as fast as she could.

She held out her hand and stopped the first car coming her way, frantically begging the driver to help her get away from the man and telling him that she had nowhere to go.

The driver was a large, black man whose face was hairy and rough. Initially, he wore a mean look, but when he saw Essie's suitcase, and the panicked look in her eyes, he smiled.

"Okay babes, jump right in. I will take care of you." Essie was not sure what he meant, but she had no choice. She tried telling herself that he could be the good Samaritan she'd prayed for. The driver's words sounded good to her. She hopped into the back of the vehicle, relieved; she was going to make it after all.

Essie introduced herself to the driver. "Sir, my name is Essie. I'm from Cascade in Hanover. What is your name, sir?"

"Big John," he barely uttered. The driver was not responsive to Essie's inquiry. It didn't seem like he was in any mood for a deep conversation, so she kept quiet, observing the passing scenery and strange, super-busy people. She felt sleepy and emotionally exhausted, and she leaned her head back and fell asleep in the car.

The man drove to a quiet, desolate area where he stopped and went to the back of the car. He intended to take full advantage of her vulnerability. By this time, his vile thoughts and dirty emotions were unstoppable. He knew that what he was about to do was wrong, but it didn't matter. His revolting life was on the wrong road anyway.

He'd spent years in prison for a similar crime. He wanted to do good this time, but he could not control himself. The opportunity presented itself to him like a cake on his birthday and he planned to take full advantage.

He had bad memories of his time in prison and he didn't wish to go back there, but he had no control over his repugnant carnal desires. He knew that he would burn in hell for his repulsive, evil deeds. He also knew, though, that he could not lay a hand upon the innocent young lady as she slept so peacefully. It was like there was a glow of light from a shining armor that shielded her from his evil thoughts. He could not bring himself to harm her. He pulled himself away out of the backseat. He went to his seat position in the front and drove off.

Chapter 6

Life is a series of successions. God never gives anyone more than they can bear. After Essie's close encounter with what could have been a terrible, life-threatening tragedy, and after her rude awakening to life in the big city, her ambitious plan came through after all.

She found a job working for a kind charming lady who was a registered nurse. The nurse had three children with her husband, a dentist. They both worked at a nearby hospital. They lived in a highly desirable, upscale neighborhood. They enjoyed an enviable upper-middle-class lifestyle in a well-appointed, two-story home.

The good-natured lady in her late thirties was Nurse Sandra Ferguson. Her refined husband, Dr. Roan Ferguson, was much older, about forty-five, and was tall, dark, handsome and cordial. They were a good-loving family.

The children's names were Lee, Jonathan, and Mary. Lee was a well-behaved boy, about five years old. Jonathan was older, around seven, and also mannerly and well behaved. Mary was the oldest child. She was nine, and shy.

The Fergusons had no luck with babysitters, but when they heard Essie's story about her awful life in the country with her adoptive parents, they decided to give her a chance. Moreover, that was their way of helping her while giving back to society.

They made Essie feel welcome in their home. They gave her a room located on the first floor. They explained to her the rules of their home and what they expected of her. They even promised to pay her a small weekly salary. In addition, Nurse Ferguson asked Essie if she knew how to cook.

"Yes, Nurse," Essie said. "I was the main cook in my family, responsible for meal preparation each night."

Essie once again reflected on her overworked life in Cascade, recognizing that it had been more of a preparation for her future than a punishment. She was happy and confident to let the Fergusons know how well she cooked. Cooking was an absolute delight for her and not considered work. Cooking was always the fun part of her day.

"Okay then Essie, along with taking care of the kids, we'll expect you to cook for us sometimes when I'm not home in time. Can you manage that?"

"Sure, nurse. No problem, mom."

Essie thanked God for placing her in this lovely family. As each day passed, she learned about the city. She wondered why she'd had to undergo such a horrific experience with that old man that chased her down before landing this job working for such a wonderful family.

Essie made up her mind then and there. She would not be intimidated by loss of hope due to the high cost or unfair price for finding out whatever good lurked behind the next door or barrier in her life. She promised to find strength from her past experiences in order to fight the unforeseeable future. She believed she deserved a good life and would not settle for anything less than the best she

26

could have. She would continue to reach high and work hard toward a good life.

Essie loved every minute of her life in Montego Bay. Although Essie was a city gal at heart, she was an avid lover of nature, and Montego Bay had lots of it to replenish her soul. After all, she was in an island where the change in seasons was marked only by newly flowering plants, blossoming trees, and the proud peacocks strutting around.

She visited Rockland's Bird Sanctuary, a bird lover's paradise. It was nested in the hills of Anchovy, just outside of Montego Bay, within the borders of the parish of St. James. She gazed at the humming bird perched on her finger while listening to the soothing sounds of their hums. She was dazzled by the Jamaican national humming bird with its stunning emerald green chest and ruby red beak. She could have watched it for hours, but instead, she strolled off the beaten path of St. James.

On another nature stroll, she observed the beautiful Montego Bay gardens complete with turquoise ponds and spectacular cascading waterfalls. Essie pitched small gravel stones into a pond full of broad green leaves floating around its edges on the surface of the waters. She watched as the water rippled outward from the core of the plunging of each stone. She smiled at the beauty of nature and frowned at the lopsided sign posted on a two-by-two stick that was planted into the ground. The sign was affixed to the top of it. The sign read: Please do not throw anything into the pond and do not feed the ducks. The tropical garden was overflowing with crotons, bamboos, ferns, cocoa plants, indigo, and forget-me-not wild macka plants.

Essie was deep in the forest as she observed the scenic backdrop of woodland and rocks. She observed the unspoiled nature of God as she continued traveling along the undeveloped dirt road. She listened to the trickling waterfalls and nearby creeks. She heard the water trickling down the bushy hillside and shady branches. She made her way through the old river bed, lush forest, and tropical foliage enveloped by green, towering trees.

Although she loved every minute of Montego Bay, she sometimes got homesick when remembering her nature getaway in the countryside of Cascade. She remembered journeying deep into the countryside through shadowed corridors and beneath tall, swaying trees. Hidden in the woodlands was the great Rocky Point River that plunged down a narrow gorge with its blue-green waters splashing along the smooth black and grey rocks of the irrigating river banks. Being in the woodland Forest never failed to give Essie a serene feeling of oneness with nature.

While living in Montego Bay, Essie never took anything for granted. She went to the beaches every possible Sunday while the Fergusons were at church. As she strolled through the busy, tourist paradise, the "Hip Strip," one of the first things that caught her eyes was the iconic aquatic playground of Jimmy Buffet's Margaritaville, where tourists and locals alike ride down an enormous waterslide and took part in other jubilant extreme water sports.

She continued along the stretch of vintage hotels, some remodeled to look modern, as she observed the island lovers sunbathing and enjoying themselves. In an effort to see more of the city, she would volunteer to do the shopping for the family and run any other errands.

While strolling through the city, she observed the crowded, colorful and lively setting of the central city streets. The crowd was a culmination of a revitalizing and industrious second city of Jamaica. It was second in size and activity to the first city, Kingston. Although Montego Bay was famous for its beaches, gourmet restaurants, and nightlife, it had an industrious side.

It was exhilarating for Essie to see the exquisite Jamaican/Spanish architecture in the central parade. It was an overpowering presence of an iconic historic site. It was Sam Sharpe Square, a friendly cobblestoned hub of activity. It was the meeting place of all the towns' people and taxi cabs. It showcased a cage that was formally a jail for runaway slaves, and the ruins of the courthouse, built in 1804 and destroyed by fire a few decades ago but now rebuilt to restore its charming beauty.

As she strolled down the streets, she noticed the architecture on both sides. They were mixed with the previous century's "gingerbread" wood houses interspersed with modern buildings.

She observed the crowded street as it hosted the country folks who flocked in to visit the markets, shops, and banks. These were some of the same country folks from Cascade who made their way by way of those dilapidated buses. The streets also hosted the guests from hotels and cruise ships as they made their way to inbond shops and crafts markets. It also hosted housewives, office girls, churchgoers giving street testimonials, and street hagglers.

Essie strolled through the local market where they sold natural produce. Country folks spread out all over the crowded, sometimes untidy street, that stretched three to four blocks long. The whole market area was full of homemade vending stalls. She observed the venders squatting, seemingly on the ground, or on low stools with their baskets full of produce between their open legs as they beckoned her to patronize their businesses. The sweet, sometimes rotten and pungent scent of overripe mangoes and bananas was heavy in the air. The local market was full of customers testing and tasting guenips, and sweet and sour saps, and nesberries.

Cars tried to get through the almost-blocked streets. Essie enjoyed the fun of haggling prices before buying her yellow yams, cassavas, and sweet potatoes.

In the city, trusted friends don't come easily. However, Essie made a few along the way. One of them was Stedman. Another was Cherry, who was Essie's age, a typical Jamaican, dark skinned and average looking, but a supportive and attentive friend.

Stedman was a handsome Indian-Jamaican boy, brown skinned and about four years older than Essie. He was a kindhearted person with a great sense of humor. Essie looked forward to meeting them on the beach every Sunday.

She decided to take personal advantage of her time off instead of going to church. She would make plans with Stedman or Cherry for things they would do or places they would go the following week.

They made an effort to visit a different beach each week. Sometimes, they would go to the park to watch a soccer game or enjoy whatever entertainment was being held. Essie developed a love beaches as well as the exciting game of soccer. She did not understand the rules well, but she loved the quick action and it was obvious when a goal was made. She couldn't explain much more than that, but she loved the game.

One Sunday, Essie and her friends arranged to meet at Doctor's Cave Beach. Stedman was the first to arrive and hurried to wade into the water, frolicking in the soothing sea.. He floated on a large inner tube pulled from an old truck tire, arms on either side of it, head bobbing in the center. He stayed close to the shore, the tips of his toes barely touching the sand. Stedman paddled around in circles, swooping down the face of the waves.

He was having a great time when he saw Essie arrive. By this time, she had evolved into a beautiful young lady. She had the figure of Raquel Welsh, the movie star. She wore a one-piece, black bathing suit and a white towel draped over her shoulders.

"Hey girl. I'm over here," Stedman said as he waved to Essie.

"I saw you Steddy. I saw you as soon as I came through the gate. I saw your little head in the middle of your big black tube. You look like a black eyed pea in a large pot." Essie dropped her towel on the sand and ran across the beach toward Stedman. She stopped abruptly at the water's edge and looked down as if she saw something strange.

"What is it Essie?"

"Oh, it's a little bitsy sea crab crawling on the sand. It's so cute. I'm going to pick it up."

"Leave the poor crab alone."

"No! I like to catch them and put them in glass and admire God's handiwork."

"But you don't have a bottle."

"That is true Steddy, you're right. I should leave it alone."

"Why don't you come into the water? It's so warm and nice."

"No, it's not. It's cold. You are lying, Steddy." Essie tested the water with her foot.

"Essie, I'm not lying. It's warm where I am. Remember, you have to dip your whole body into the water first and then you'll see that it's really warm."

"You know, a friend of mine used to say; 'Never test the water with both feet.'"

"Or else what?"

"Or else you'll get burned or drown, or whatever. It's just a saying or an old phrase or proverb. Don't get technical with me, Steddy."

"Okay, Miss Pretty, I'll leave you and your country phrases alone. Soon you'll be telling me that one hand of a banana is better than two bunches," Stedman said with a grin.

"Are you teasing me, Steddy? You know I don't like to be called country. I'm a big city girl like everyone else now," Essie protested against Stedman's unwelcome humor.

"Okay, big city girl."

"Where is Cherry?" Essie asked, realizing that Stedman played alone.

"I don't know. She's not here as yet."

"I hope she comes. I could kill her if she doesn't show up like last Sunday," Essie said sarcastically.

"Talking about the devil, there she comes through the gate," Stedman said as he spotted Cherry in a pink, two-piece bathing suit and a white towel around her waist.

"Oh great, here she comes."

"Yes, Miss Miserable is here."

"No, she's not. Leave my friend alone," Essie said.

"Hey, bad-minded people, I can hear you. You're talking bad things about me. You all can't stand to see a girl make a grand entrance. Yuh done know. A mi dat," Cherry called out to her friends (in her Jamaican dialect) as she approached them.

"Oh no, Cherry, not me. Steddy is calling you miserable."

"Stedman? Let him gwane. You don't see it's a big trouble maker dat? He needs a big lick inna him head." Cherry threatened (in her dialect) as she joined them in the water. Both Essie and Cherry playfully held on to one side of Stedman's tube as they mischievously tried to hoist him out of it. They spent the rest of their time playing and catching up on the past week's events.

"Cherry, what happened to you last week?" Essie asked.

33

"Nothing. Just some schoolwork that I needed to catch up on."

"Mo Bay High School is getting tougher these days," Stedman joined the girls in conversation.

"Yes, sir. I can't wait to finish that school. They give too much extra schoolwork on the weekends. Dem trying fi kill mi marsa."

"I need to go back to school one of these days so I can go on to college," Essie confessed her dreams to her friends.

"That's a good idea," Cherry said.

"You know, I went to a cricket match the other day. It was very good," Stedman said as he tried to steer the conversation in a different direction. He never was much of a school type and started working in the hotel industry at seventeen.

"Where was the game?" Cherry asked.

"At Jarrett Park."

"Who was playing?" Essie, also curious, asked about the game.

"It was a big match, man. It was the West Indies playing Pakistan. It was a kind of test match," Stedman explained it to the girls.

"Is it still going on?" Cherry said.

"No, it was just a three-day match. It's finished now."

"Wow. I wished I'd known about it," Essie's voice was, low with regret.

"But Essie, you don't like cricket, you like soccer," Stedman said in an effort to remind her that cricket was not her favorite sport.

"Essie doesn't know what she likes, Stedman," Cherry exclaimed.

"Yes, I do. I like cricket a lot, but I love soccer more."

"Okay, next time I'll tell you about it in advance. Oh, and by the way, there's a big soccer match next week at Jarrett Park. We could go there next Sunday."

"Okay, I'm in," said Essie.

"Who is playing?" Cherry asked, making sure it was worth her time.

"Some team from Kingston's supposed to play Montego Bay Soccer Club."

"Oh, that should be good. I'm in, too," Cherry promised to join her friends at the upcoming game.

"What time is the match?"

"Starts around 4 p.m."

"Where do you want to get together?" Cherry asked Stedman.

"How about at the front gate? My good friend will be working there so we won't have to pay to get in," Stedman assured them.

As day drew to a close, the three turned their thoughts on meeting the following Sunday.

At eighteen, Essie was enjoying her life. For the first time, she felt it was worth living and she embraced life to its fullest. She felt confident and it showed. Her one regret was not completing her schooling before running away from Cascade. If she'd done so, she could take advantage of the many opportunities the big city offered. She could have continued her studies in Montego Bay and moved on to college to obtain a professional career.

Her eyes had opened to the ways of the world and she wanted more, including bigger and better dreams. She was well aware of her beauty, but she knew her looks could only get her but so far. On the other hand, if she had a good education, she could secure a bright future for herself. Thus, she started planning to return to school as soon as possible.

As time progressed, Stedman and Essie grew closer. One Sunday, while at the beach, they even confronted each other about the direction of their casual relationship. It was at a secluded spot facing the golden sunset where they lay on the sand laughing and having fun. Eventually, Stedman started telling her how he truly felt and that he'd love her to be his girlfriend.

Essie had been attracted to him all along but was afraid to let him know. The pleasant news was like sweet music to her ears, as she listened to Stedman say how much he loved and desired her. She leaned over and softly kissed his lips. "I was hoping you'd say that."

"Believe it or not, I was attracted to you from the first day that I laid eyes on you at Sunset Beach Place, but I didn't have the guts to tell you until now. Essie, I loved you then. I've loved you all along. I love you now and I'll love you forever."

"Wow! Four years is a long time," Essie exclaimed with a confident, flirtatious smile. It felt good to be loved. It gave her chills to hear those words from Stedman. In a sinful world of fornication and blissful ignorance, they made love on the white sands of Cornwall Beach Place.

Chapter 7

Essie's favorite food was the Jamaican national dish, which was made of akee combined with pieces of cod. The two are combined in a Dutch pot or deep frying pan to be simmered down with various seasonings, including onion, black pepper, tomatoes, and a little hot sauce. Essie loved her akee and salt fish with a variety of side dishes, but her favorite was plain white rice. To her it was a tantalizing combination. It was most delightful, and she would give anything in exchange for her favorite meal.

Therefore, it was a surprise when she turned down the Fergusons' offer to have dinner with them one evening.

Essie diligently prepared the dinner of akee and salt fish and presented it at the table, but she declined to join the family for dinner. That was unusual and caused Nurse Ferguson to inquire about her health.

"Essie, my dear child, are you feeling okay?"

"Yes, Nurse Ferguson."

"You never turn away from your favorite dish. What's wrong?"

"Nothing, I just don't feel like eating it today."

"What are you going to eat instead?"

"I'll just eat a piece of bread and a pear for now, and maybe later I'll have some plain rice with butter."

"Okay, suit yourself child. All I know is that something is not right."

Essie also wondered what was wrong with her. She couldn't imagine turning down her favorite meal but she had no appetite for akee. The sight and smell of it made her nauseous.

For the next few weeks, Nurse Ferguson noticed that Essie's behavior had changed significantly. She slept an awful lot, often forgetting to do chores around the house, and spent excessive time in her bedroom. She even forgot to pick Mary up from school one evening as instructed. This oversight caused chaos and panic.

Nurse Ferguson was very upset and called Essie aside and told her that she had to leave. Essie was fired from the best job she ever had. Sadness overwhelmed her, followed by confusion and loss; she didn't know what to do, but admitted they were right. She knew her work performance was no longer acceptable, but she just couldn't seem to do much about it. Her body was changing. She'd gained significant weight and tired more quickly. She called Cherry to see if she could help her with a place to stay until she could get another job.

Cherry, who lived with her parents, asked them if her friend could stay a few days at their home. They agreed, saying it was all right as long as it was only for a few days. Essie was grateful.

They packed her belongings at the Fergusons' and went to Cherry's home. Essie was confused, unsure where to go or what to do next.

On the same afternoon they moved to Cherry's home, Essie fell to the ground carrying a box to the bedroom. Cherry saw her fall and started yelling.

"Help! Mommy! Daddy! Help! Essie fainted." Cherry feared it was due to exhaustion. Cherry's parents rushed downstairs and saw Essie lying on the ground. They rushed her to the hospital. It was there the doctors diagnosed her with a three-month miscarriage.

Essie thought, *Maybe Nurse Ferguson knew it all along. That could be the real reason why she fired me. She did not want to be bothered with a maternal situation on the job.* Essie, being young and unmarried, had not planned for a baby, but to know she'd just lost one made her sad.

When Stedman heard, he was also sad because he would have loved to have his first child with a pretty girl like Essie. He rushed to the hospital to see her. When he got there, she was in tears. "Stedman, I'm sorry I lost your baby."

"Essie my love, don't cry. I love you and I want you to come and live with me and we'll have another baby, get married, and be a family," Stedman comforted her. Essie hugged him and cried on his shoulders.

Chapter 8

Living with Stedman was Essie's first step toward maturity and independence. The topic of marriage never came up again, but Essie did not bother to aggravate what she considered to be a wonderful life with Stedman. She believed in the proverb that stated, "what's not broken don't try to fix it." Each day, she learned more about herself and how to please him.

"Hello! I'm home."

"Hey Steddy! How was work today?" Essie always met Stedman at the door with a warm hug and a long, welcoming kiss. She gave Stedman a welcome fit for a king and he loved every minute of it.

"Work was okay. There's nothing special to talk about. It was just another hard day working for the money."

"Did you get any tips today?"

"Yes, but not much."

"Okay, honey. Just sit on the chair. I'll get your shoes off for you."

"Thank you Essie, my dear. I thought about you all day long. I couldn't wait to get home to see you. I missed you so much."

"I have a surprise for you, Steddy." Essie stooped down to untie his shoes.

"Essie, do you know you really rock my world?"

"Come with me." Essie rose and put his shoes away in the corner. She then took his hand and led him to the dining area. "Surprise!"

"Wow! You did all that for me? Essie you are so romantic. I really love it." Stedman admired the large bouquet of flowers on the dining table with a bottle of wine sitting in the ice bucket. The table was nicely decorated with burning candles and red and white rose petals all around the edge of the table. It was a breathtaking sight to behold. "But what's the occasion?"

"We're celebrating our love today. That's all."

"So why aren't you dressed up? This seems like more than an informal dinner celebration. It's a first for me, but I like it."

"This is my style, my way of celebrating our love. Have a seat and I'll fetch the food from the kitchen. I've already prepared it."

Essie dashed to the kitchen for the food while Stedman took a seat. She always made him feel like a king, having learned early on that a happy home makes a happy life. She did her best to make sure that he was happy at home. She could not control what went on at work, but she could make his homelife pleasant.

"I prepared your favorite-- oxtail with rice and peas." Essie rushed back with his hot plate of food trailing a familiar sweet smelling aroma as she made her way to the table. It stimulated his nostrils and his appetite as it filled the air. Stedman was in bliss. He had his favorite meal and his beautiful girlfriend at a special romantic occasion at home.

What more could a man ask for in life, short of the grace of God?

They were in love and it showed. Essie gave all her love and affection to Stedman and he gave her no less in return. She felt loved and secure with him. Stedman had a comfortable, two - bedroom apartment in the upscale downtown area of Baldwin Heights and Essie was delighted to share his home and his life.

He was a skillfully trained waiter in a popular hotel called Half Moon Resort. His pay was not great, but he sometimes made quite a bundle in tips. Therefore, he could afford a decent lifestyle for them. This also meant he was willing and able to take care of her and a child or two if they came along.

Indeed, Stedman confessed to Essie that he would love to have two or three kids before he turned twenty-five. His dad always told him that was the best time to have one's first set of kids, and was the main reason why he started working at seventeen. Starting so young and working so hard assured that he could afford a nice home and have a decent savings in the bank to start a family.

He loved kids and he wished to have some of his own, especially now that he had a beautiful woman in his life. He wasted no time trying to get Essie pregnant again.

Essie got pregnant within nine months of moving in with Stedman and this time she knew it, having educated herself on the signs. Essic did everything right to the best of her knowledge. She ate properly and got plenty of rest. She visited her doctor twice to make sure everything was good with the baby. That was more than the average expectant mother in that era.

It was a ghastly surprise, therefore, when she had a miscarriage in her fifth month while taking a bath at home. Essie was shocked and couldn't understand how a stillbirth could happen unprovoked. She started blaming herself, thinking that she was not made to bear children. She feared it was not God's plan for her. Essie thought everything negative a woman could think. At nineteen, she knew her age wasn't the problem. There were many girls that were younger than her, having children with no such problem.

Stedman came home from work that day to find her in tears. Heartbroken, she told him the miserable news. By now, Essie knew how badly Stedman wanted her to have his child and she felt sorry for him.

Stedman calmed and comforted her, saying he would always be there for her, with or without children. It didn't matter to him. It was her love that mattered most.

Stedman, however, reneged on his promise a year later when Essie got pregnant for the third time, but was unable to bring her pregnancy to term. Stedman told her that although he loved her dearly, she would have to leave his home. He had a new girlfriend who was pregnant with his child.

Essie was hurt, but she knew there was no way she could repair their relationship without bearing him children. Essie did not believe Stedman's story of another pregnant girlfriend. She believed it was a convenient excuse to get her to leave.

In the end, it didn't matter. He wanted her out of his life. He wanted kids and she could not bear them-- it was as simple as that.

Essie understood Stedman's point of view. Although she was heartbroken, she was not angry with him. Not until she discovered his story was true—he had gotten another girl pregnant.

"Steddy, how you could say you love me and cheat on me at the same time?" She was furious.

"I do. Well, I did," Stedman searched for the right answer.

"You're no good, mon, ya know dat? You're a fraud an' a no good, low down liar. I wish ya'd burn in hell," Essie shouted.

"Essie, I didn't intend for us to end up this way, but you gave me no choice."

"What? I gave you no choice?" Essie eyes blazed red as fire and her heart pounded with rage.

"You knew kids were important to me and you deceived me. You knew you couldn't have children, but you didn't tell me. Your uterus is, well... well, condemned. There I said it. It needed to be said. At first I thought it was my fault, but after three times with the same result, I had to see if I had anything to do with you losing my babies. That is why I took Cherry up on her offer. I needed to know that I can have healthy kids just like everyone else," Stedman said.

"Cherry? Oh my God! No! My friend Cherry? I cannot believe my ears." Essie was stunned. Cherry and Stedman were having a baby? She was beyond angry now. She staggered out the door, then ran around to the back of their apartment building, and started to sob.

Essie became depressed knowing her best friend and her lover had betrayed her in such a despicable way. It was the worst feeling she had felt. It hurt to lose her first love, but she knew she'd get over him. However, it was different losing her best friend at the same time and in that way. Who could she go to now? To whom would she turn for help and comfort if not God? When Essie was young, she had learned not to trust anyone. Then she met Cherry and her feelings had changed. She'd met a real and true friend, at least that's what she had thought.

Heartsick and tried, Essie decided that she needed to find a suitable career. She pleaded with Stedman to give her some time to find a job. She remembered a magnificent cake that she'd skillfully baked for a party at Dr. Ferguson's home. She remembered how excited everyone was about the cake. It dawned on her how nice it would be to work as a chef at a good hotel.

She started looking for a job in the culinary arena. She searched all over Montego Bay and, with the help of Stedman's connections, landed her first chef job at Round Hill Hotel. After she made her first salary, she paid for a one-bedroom apartment.

Essie excelled as a chef. It was like she put her pain and sorrow into her work. Essie turned her disappointments and hurt emotions into working passion. She did well and her manager liked her skillful, enthusiastic work. Essie knew that she would be a good chef. She loved to cook and it showed in her avid excitement for a tasty meal.

If a meal was not good, she was the first to let it be known. She couldn't hold back her personal opinion about the taste of certain foods. She thought of a dish like a symphony. Each part needed to come together at the precise time and complement the other parts. Cooking was like music, where each instrument, like each ingredient, added its own beautiful sound. She believed that anyone could prepare an edible meal using good ingredients, yet only a top chef could take the same ordinary ingredients and produce an unforgettable, gourmet meal.

Essie cared about the quality of the outcome and refused to accept ordinary results. She believed in the basics, learning the details, because she believed the details resulted in a perfectly cooked roast or pitch-perfect sauce, to layering a dish with flavors. She put thought into each plate of food she prepared.

People trusted her because she had reliable taste buds and a unique and discerning personal taste. When a meal was good, she would make open remarks about it, praising the chef or whoever provided the meal. Everyone who knew Essie knew she was obsessed with food.

It surprised no one when she became a popular, noteworthy chef. Although enthralled by the culinary fine arts, she never went to school to study it. Her ability was a natural skill. Essie did, however, further her culinary education by various cook books from the library. She loved to try a new recipe and would spread the book open in the kitchen and start making the new dish, while humming a song to herself. She enjoyed every minute of cooking.

When she was in the kitchen, she was more entertaining than the popular Emeril television cooking show but without the *"bam!"* and the juggling knives. To Essie, being a chef was more fun and excitement than work. She was promoted to head chef in a short time at Round Hill Hotel. Essie had discovered her hidden talent and began to let it shine. She had few regrets about her turbulent breakup with Stedman. She was grateful for the day that she had been forced to go out and seek a job because it helped her find her real, God-given gift and talent in life.

Chapter 9

Although Essie was thrilled by discovering her newfound culinary career, which was like finding gold in a hidden treasure box, every now and then, she would have a sad spell. Sometimes she would sit in the corner by herself, feeling sad about how life had started so unfairly for her. More than anything, she had a growing concern about her sterility problem. She felt cursed by God by not being able to have children. Worse, she worried that she would always be shunned by men for being sterile. To ease her anxiety, Essie began smoking cigarettes. "It just feels right. It helped me to think more clearly during my sad mood swings," she would say.

One day, while on her daily errands, Essie decided to take a cigarette break. After finding a pleasant spot, she sat on the wall and gazed over the town. Deep in thought and reflecting on how her life was going, she was interrupted when a minister walked up to her, seemingly from out of nowhere, and introduced himself.

"Hello, pretty young lady. My name is Reverend Paul Murray. What's yours?"

"Essie, sir," she replied cordially, a bewildered look on her face.

"You look a bit sad today."

"I am okay, sir."

"Tell me, my child, what's on your mind?" the reverend insisted.

Essie took a good look at the well-mannered and handsome, black, middle-aged minister.

"Are you the pastor at Holy Cross Church of God in Mount Salem?"

"Yes, my dear child. Have you ever been to my church?"

"Yes, sir, Essie said. "I attended your Easter ceremony last year."

"Really?"

"I went with Nurse Ferguson and her family."

"Great. I'm very happy to hear you attended my church once before; but Miss Essie, it doesn't have to be an Easter celebration for you to attend my church service."

"I know, sir."

"I would like you to pay us a visit next Sunday if you can."

Essie thought for a while then responded with a request of her own. "Pastor, I have a question for you."

"What is it my child?"

"Why am I cursed by God?"

"No! No! Never say that again, my child. That is not true. You are a special child of God. If you were not special, He would not have sent me here to talk with you today."

"Well, if I'm so special, why can't I have children?"

The reverend closed his eyes and turned his face upward in a dramatic way as he offered a quick, whispered prayer to God. "Do you believe in God, my child?"

49

"Yes, sir," she said without hesitation.

"Well, let's go somewhere and talk about this matter. Where do you live? Is it close by?"

"Yes, sir."

The reverend stood up, turned to look around, wanting to ensure their privacy. It was as if he was about to do or say the unforgivable.

"The Lord is telling me right now that I should touch you so you can be healed."

Those words sounded good to Essie's ears and she nodded several times. "Yes, pastor, I live near here," she said, relief and joy on her face.

"Let me take you home."

Essie led the way to her house.

They held hands and prayed, and after the short prayer session, Rev. Murray turned to her. "Essie, my child, do you believe in God?"

"Yes, sir."

"Essie, my child, do you believe in miracles?"

"Yes, sir."

"Then my child, take off those worldly, condemned clothes you're wearing and let me heal you through the grace of God."

Essie was shocked to hear those words from the good minister, but believed she had nothing to lose. So she obeyed him and undressed, except for her underwear.

"All of it, my dear child, all of it. Take off all your sinful, forsaken clothes," he said, shouting in a demanding tone.

"Okay, Reverend," Essie reluctantly complied.

50

"Essie, you are like a pretty, unspoiled flower that was planted in rough terrain or by the wayside. Do you believe in God?"

This time she did not respond, so the reverend continued.

"Essie, my child, do you believe in miracles?"

Essie started to laugh, ripples of mirth burst from her throat, a kind of laughter that was very unique to Essie; strong, loud and seemingly endless.

"Pastor, get on with your business at hand."

"Well then, kindly turn your back to me," he said, in a soft and provocative voice. He altered his tone so it would match the command he needed. Essie did what the minister said without question. The ordained man approached her.

"Oh, Lord! Oh, Lord! Thank you for choosing me today to do Thy work. Praise be to God in the most high. Thank you, Lord. Thank you, Lord. Thank you, Lord."

Chapter 10

Aristotle once said, "A tyrant must put on the appearance of uncommon devotion to religion. Subjects are less apprehensive of illegal treatment from a ruler whom they consider God-fearing and pious. On the other hand, they do less easily move against him, believing that he has the Gods on his side."

After Essie's strange and eerie encounter with Rev. Murray, her faith in God became more questionable than ever and she was confused. She didn't understand what had happened to her and she concluded it was just another bizarre occurrence in her life.

However, when she missed her menstruation the following month, Essie started believing again. She believed, it was a miracle of God and that this time, she would bring the pregnancy to term. She felt happy again but hesitated to raise her hopes too high.

Essie decided to tell Rev. Murray the good news, but the only way she knew of getting in touch with him was by going to his church. Essie decided to attend services on the following Sunday with the hope of speaking to him. She knew she'd have to be discreet about such an abnormal, almost religiously fanatic situation. As she thought about how strange the situation was, a chilling feeling ripped through her body. She felt like a religious groupie chasing after a celebrity.

She went to church as planned, and at the end of service, was informed by one of the deacons that the reverend had migrated to Canada with his wife and kids. Essie realized that the reverend knew he was leaving the island so he got his kicks on, with her, a naïve girl. He was like all the other men who would say or do anything to get under a female's dress.

Essie realized that she would have to this pregnancy and baby by herself. Even though it would be difficult, she was content with what she considered to be a trade-off with God. God gave her a baby, but the baby would not have a father. She accepted her fate and was ready to step up to the plate and be both mother and father to her miracle baby.

The only fear Essie had was how to deal with work and her bills in the final stage of her pregnancy. The answer came to her when she met "Longman," one of her coworkers. His real name was Richard Browdie. He was called Longman because he was tall and skinny, a handsome, light-skinned, charming chap in his late twenties.

Longman discovered that Essie was pregnant after speaking to her at work. He'd always admired her beauty and her strict work ethic and had wanted to approach her earlier, but was too timid to do so. By the time he speak to her on a personal basis, he was disappointed to find out that he had made his move too late. Another man had obviously beaten him to the punch.

However, as they continued talking, he realized that the baby's father would not be in Essie's life. This gave him some hope. He knew that he cared enough about Essie to date her even with one child. Although, he really wished that the baby was his, he and Essie grew to be friends and lovers for the next four months. By this time, Essie's pregnancy became obvious and a grave concern to her manager.

One day, Longman went on his lunch break and saw Essie in tears. The manager was pressuring her to quit her job due to her pregnancy and slow productivity. Longman encouraged her to quit her job and live with him in his one-bedroom apartment on the other side of town. They were already dating anyway so he thought he might as well take on the full responsibility of being a father to her baby and build a serious relationship with her. He promised to take care of her and that she would not have to worry about anything. Essie was comforted by Longman's thoughtful words.

Eventually she took his advice and quit her job. She moved in with him during her seventh month of pregnancy.

The small apartment was a little tight for her and Longman. She worried about how it would work out when the baby came. She was concerned about the space, but was relieved and happy that at least she and her baby would have a roof over their heads and someone to take care of them.

When the baby was born, Longman was thrilled and supportive, as he promised. He was a good father to the baby, even though he decided not to let her carry his last name. Instead, he encouraged Essie to name the baby after the reverend. Together, they decided to name the miracle baby Gena Murray because she was a pretty, black-skinned girl. Essie chose Gena, a shortened form of Genie, because a genie is a supernatural spirit that can take human form to serve the person who calls on it. Essie believed that God had sent Gena to her and that she was her miracle baby, the answer to her dreams.

Essie was happy with her baby and with her relationship with Longman. She had one growing concern with Longman, though. He was a nice guy and an excellent provider, but he had a drinking problem that was growing worse with time.

After eight months of living with him, he began to come home on Friday nights, his payday, noisy and roaring drunk. Essie paid no attention until one night, very drunk, he demanded that she leave his house immediately. He told her that she had to take her precious baby with her, but he only said it because he got upset with Essie.

He believed that Essie preferred the baby over him and his needs. Saying that for all he'd done for her and the baby, the least she could do was pay him more attention.

Essie calmed him down, but from that time onward, she knew in her heart that a stupefied, staggering drunk was no father for her baby girl. She was hit by embarrassment too many times. This time she was not willing to turn the other cheek. This was not the way she wanted to live, nor was it the way she wanted her daughter to grow up.

Essie began making plans and the second time Longman came home woozy, drunk, and rowdy, demanding she do whatever he said or leave his house, she assured him they would leave soon. She redoubled her efforts at finding a job, and by luck and chance, met Mr. Allen, a popular barber who had his own business and was doing well for himself.

Chapter 11

Essie sat on a bench in the middle of downtown Montego Bay. She'd pulled her hair back and combed it into a long ponytail and her tiny feet wore a pair of cute, white pumps. She smiled in a flirtatious manner as she watched Mr. Allen approach her.

Mr. Allen was flattered, wondering what good deed he'd done to deserve such a pretty young girl flirting with him. Their eyes met and they smiled at each other. Essie sat upright as Mr. Allen walked over to her. "Hello, young lady. What's your name?"

"Essie; and yours?"

"I am John Allen. I own the barbershop down the street."

"Oh really? I know where it is. I've passed by there many times."

"Could I offer you some lunch at the hillside plaza? I'd planned to eat alone, but I'd much prefer the company of a pretty young lady like you. Would you join me?"

"Sure. Why not?"

The lunch date went well and the time spent after lunch was even better. They went for a walk by the ocean and picked a private spot where they stopped to chat. They spent all afternoon getting to know each other and the evening ended with a kiss. They made arrangements to meet the next day.

Not long after Essie met John Allen Sr., they engaged in a serious relationship and she moved from Longman's apartment into his home. John was a noble, sincere family man with two kids of his own. He was fresh out of a divorce and had lost custody of his kids to his ex-wife in a hefty divorce agreement. The settlement was enough for his ex-wife and kids to live a comfortable life. Therefore, he had no guilt in starting his life over with someone else, even with someone who already had a child that was not his own. He was a handsome man, light-skinned, conscientious, intelligent, and in his early forties.

There was one outstanding aspect about John's appearance. He had beautiful wavy hair. Being a barber and the owner of a busy shop in the heart of Montego Bay, he kept his hair neat and attractive at all times. Any woman would have been happy to have him father her children and Essie was no exception. Within a month of living with John, she got pregnant with her second child, whom they named Junior J. Allen.

As Junior grew older, his looks became more pronounced, mirroring John Allen, right down to his beautiful wavy hair. John was confident and happy about his first male child. He loved him very much, but being the intelligent father that he was, he showed equal love and attention to both Junior and Gena.

About nine months after Junior's birth, Essie conceived another child. She delivered the baby the day after Christmas in 1953. This time it was a pretty baby girl who looked just like Essie. They named her Betty Allen. John was proud of his new family. He felt like he had regained everything that he had lost to his ex-wife. He now had a prettier, younger, and kinder woman in his life with three beautiful kids. He took them everywhere he went because they were his pride and joy. Essie made John a very happy man.

Essie, in turn, was happy until John's terrible ex-wife, Audrey, came back into their lives. Out of jealousy, Audrey began causing trouble in their relationship. Audrey became angry and evil when she noticed how proud and happy John was with his new family. She could not bear to see him so happy with his new life and independence.

Audrey started sending her kids over to John with various mischievous and demanding requests. Suddenly, she wanted to force the kids back into his life, in order to cause trouble. Although John loved all his kids, both his three kids by Essie and his two daughters by Audrey, he did not let his ex-wife's plan disrupt his newfound happiness.

When Audrey realized that she couldn't disrupt his life by manipulating the kids, she started verbally attacking Essie and even threatened to fight her if she saw her on the streets. Essie tried to ignore her, but Audrey kept on bothering her. Essie got fed up. She battle within herself against the devil. She believed she was fighting good against evil. She was hit by her own fear, as well as the envy and jealousy of John's ex-wife.

Essie was pushed from behind through the front door of her relationship by Audrey's covetousness.

On top of everything, Essie heard rumors through the grapevine that John had been having an affair with a lady that visited his barbershop. Essie and John began having problems in their relationship.

Their relationship suffered and Essie decided to accept an offer made to her by a man she had met while shopping one day. He was a rich businessman named Conroy Levy, who lived out of town. He offered to take care of her and her three kids by getting an apartment for her in Montego Bay. When he was in town, he would have a family and a place he could call his second home. Although she knew it was going to hurt John badly, she took Conroy Levy's offer and moved to her own apartment, subsidized completely by Conroy Levy.

This arrangement worked well for Essie because she felt more independent. Moreover, she only saw Conroy Levy once a month when he came into town to do business. When he was in town, Essie attended to his every need.

"Hello, sweetheart. How was your drive into town?"

"It was tiresome, my dear. Thank you for asking." She stood in the doorway.

"Come in. Let me have your shoes. The kids are with a friend of mine so we are alone." She turned around and led Conroy inside to the living room and removed his shoes. "I missed you, sweetheart. I've been preparing for your arrival."

"I see. The apartment looks clean and neat."

"Yes, all for you, my love."

When Conroy was in town, he would stay for three or four days at most. He was happy to have a pretty woman like Essie to spend time with. It was more than worth it for Conroy.

After about a year together, Essie got pregnant form Conroy. They named the girl baby Lela Levy. Not long after her birth, Essie turned Lela over to her cousin, Miriam, who lived in Mt. Salem, a popular district in Montego Bay. Miriam offered to help her with the child and support her, so Essie let her have the baby as an unofficial adoption with the genuine intention to get her back at a later time in life. Miriam had difficulties having children of her own, so she was happy to care for baby Lela.

Chapter 12

Conroy Levy agreed to the unofficial adoption. He understood that it would be less of a financial burden on both Essie and him. Lela Levy had a strong resemblance to her father, who was in no way a handsome fellow.

Because Conroy was wealthy, he bought Essie a nice, used, pearl-black Chevrolet, even before she had a license to drive. Essie didn't mind not having a license because she was able to employ someone to drive it for her. Whenever she planned to do her errands, she would call her driver and be transported wherever she wanted to go. Essie started enjoying the high society lifestyle of being Conroy's second lady. She loved it, and for the first time, she felt that life was fair. She even found a way to make extra money when Conroy was away. She used her car as a taxi cab and her driver ran a regular route. The driver made a salary for himself and gave Essie the difference in profit each week.

This arrangement worked well for Essie until the driver had an accident and the car was declared a total loss. When Conroy heard about the incident, he became upset with Essie for using the vehicle as a taxi without telling him. He felt betrayed and stopped visiting Essie when he was in the area. He stopped sending money or child support. She was hit by disappointment and regrets.

Essie did everything she could to try and reach him with messages and letters, but he did not respond.

Luckily, she had the forethought to put the extra cash she'd made from her taxi business in the bank. But the money didn't last long. She started looking for employment as a cook in various hotels and private resorts. Due to her excellent recommendation from Round Hill Hotel, she got a job at Chatham Resort. She employed a friend, Vera, to help her with the kids.

By this time, Essie also developed a drinking habit and an increased smoking habit. If anyone asked her why she drank, she would say she drank what it took to put her to sleep. There were too many thoughts running through her head at night that prevented her from sleeping. She would make her daily trip to the rum bar on her way from work. There she would order a quarter quart of Jamaican White Rum, which she would take home. Before bedtime, she would drink the full quantity in one sitting, two at most.

On her way to the rum bar, she met her next lover, Mr. Leonard Williams. He was also a frequent visitor to the same bar, a scholar, and once highly respected lawyer in Montego Bay. He was a popular figure although he was not a handsome man. He was wealthy and had a great personality. Due to his popularity, he could get any girl he wanted and usually chose the prettiest and most desirable ladies in town.

Leonard charmed Essie and won her over. They had a brief relationship, but when Essie realized he was an uncontrollable alcoholic, she broke off the relationship. At least, that was what

Essie thought. In reality, she ended the despicable relationship a little too late. She missed her period the following month and was pregnant by the alcoholic lawyer. Essie received a blow of disappointment which hurt her because she had not seen it coming. She was not happy with the news, but there was no choice. She would never abort a healthy child. Moreover, because of how difficult it was for her to have her first child, she promised herself that she would never abort any of her pregnancies. When the baby was born one day after Christmas, December 26, 1957, she named the baby girl Myrtle Williams.

With five children to feed and care for by herself, with a big assist from her cousin Miriam, who helped with Lela, she started working two jobs. She worked in the mornings at the Chatham Hotel Resort and at night at Verne Hill Resort. She juggled the two jobs so she could maintain a roof over her kids' heads and provide them food.

On weekends she did the grocery shopping. She had a tight budget, so she went to the food market because the food was known to be fresher and less expensive. One weekend she went to buy yams from a vendor and a strange thing happened. After she chose the yams and some mangoes, the man weighed the food, put them in a bag, and gave it to her. "Here, this is from me to you, my pretty lady."

"Thank you, sir, but what is the cost?"

"Nothing, my pretty lady," the kind vender replied, as if giving things away was not a big deal to him.

"Thank you. God bless you, sir."

She thought that it was strange because no one gave anything away for free. However, she smiled and walked away. The next day, while at home relaxing and reminiscing on the kind deed that came her way, it dawned on her that she remembered the face of the vendor. She recognized his eyes and his smile but she could not, for the life of her, remember where they met before. It bothered her all week, so much so that she could not wait to go back the following weekend to meet this person again and to find out how she knew him.

Saturday morning bright and early, Essie hurried to the market, more to satisfy her curiosity than to purchase groceries. She rushed to the same spot where the kind gentleman had been, but he was not there. Baffled and perturbed, she circled around the area many times as she shopped, but, he was not there. Essie checked with the nearby vendors, but no one recognized the person Essie described.

After a whole day of inquiry, she gave up and went home, vowing to return every weekend until she found out who the kind man was.

Three weekends later, Essie found the vendor whose identity bewildered her, and not knowing what to say, went to him and ordered the same things she'd ordered on the previous occasion. The vendor did the same thing, and after weighing the food, he put her produce in a bag and gave it to her.

"Here, my pretty lady. This is from me to you."

"Thank you, sir, but I want to know why you're giving me this food for free?"

"You remind me of a good friend I once had. She was special to me, so by giving you this gift, it is like giving it to her."

"What was her name?"

"Essie Streete," he said, not expecting much reaction. What could it mean to her anyway? He tossed the name out casually, although it meant the world to him.

All of a sudden, it came to her and she let out a shrill scream of surprise, causing a stir in the market as people wondered what was wrong.

Her whole body quivered as she realized she knew him and from where. *Tim!* It all came together-- the eyes, the familiar smile; he was her old friend from childhood. She was fourteen again, living back in the countryside of Cascade and barely speaking to anyone in her jealous and abusive family. Tim was her only friend. He would walk her home from school in the evenings and listen to her talk about her unfair treatment by her adopted family.

Tim was sixteen at the time, very black skinned and handsome, and felt privileged to be Essie's friend. He knew he was not the brightest child in school and planned on quitting at time. Essie convinced him to stay in school. He agreed, but only because it meant he got to walk her home from school.

One day, Tim saw her standing at the public pipe in Cascade waiting in line to get her bucket filled with water.

"Hey, Essie, you're out early this morning, I see." Tim greeted his little friend with a warm, happy-to-see-you hug.

"Oh yeah, I have to fill the three water drums at home, so I thought I'd get an early start," Essie said. Her cheerful tone indicated she was happy to see her friend. It was wonderful to meet him on the road.

"Really?"

"Can you believe it?"

"Three large drums?"

"Three huge drums."

"That small bucket will take forever, Essie. I could take a slow boat to China and back, and you would still be here filling dem drums."

"You can say that again. I'll never finish today, but it's as much as I can manage. I couldn't find a big one, so I took the first bucket without a leak in it."

"Essie, I've got an idea. Let me run home to fetch a larger bucket so I can help you fill up faster."

"Oh really? Thank you, Tim. You're the best."

Tim ran home and returned with a large bucket in hand. Almost out of breath, he hurried to Essie, eager to help her, as all good friends would. He considered it a pleasure and couldn't think of anything he'd rather do. It was always a joy being around Essie. He looked forward to meeting her on the streets, or at the shops, or even at her gate.

Aunt Rose would not let him come into their yard, so he would sometimes wait outside, just hoping to get a glimpse of Essie. Many times he thought of visiting her at home, but he was afraid she would get in trouble.

Tim believed in the phrase: "never test the water with both feet." He was content just to meet Essie on her errands along the streets or at the shops.

The drums held water for both household and personal use. Because the house had no plumbing, all water needs were satisfied through the drums. On a rainy day, there was less need for getting water from the public pipes. The drums, set up in strategic locations outside of the house, collected rainwater through gutters and channeled it into the drums. Some of these gutters were made from bamboo trees and lined the top of the house on all four sides. Cascade never complained that there was too much rain. Rainwater was more than a blessing to them; it was survival.

Another time back in Cascade when Tim saw Essie was when she was on her way to the river to wash her family's dirty clothes.

"Essie, where are you going?" Tim shouted.

"To the river," Essie shouted back. He was on the other side of the road playing a game of dominoes with his friends.

"Which one?"

"I'm going to Rocky Point River."

"To do what?"

"Tim, stop bothering me. You can see the basket of dirty clothes on my head. If you want to come, just come and stop bothering me."

That was all Tim needed to hear-- Essie didn't mind his company to the river. He ran across the street to meet her.

"All the way to Rocky Point River? That's very far, but I'll come anyway."

"You know you want to come, Tim, so don't pretend."

"That's a lot of clothes, Essie. That basket is really big." Tim nodded at the overloaded, brown plastic basket, so full of dirty clothes that a variety of items hung out of the packed container. Essie skillfully leaned the basket to one side of her head, a well-wrapped piece of clothing provided a buffer between her head and the basket. She looked like a typical country girl. This caused Tim to admire her even more.

"Yeah it is. Are you going to help me with it?"

"No! Are you crazy, Essie?"

"Why not, Tim? Are you not my friend anymore?"

"Yes, but my friends will laugh at me."

"Laugh? Why?" Essie pretended ignorance, but she knew that he was right. Boys were brutal to each other when it come to those types of manly myths. She figured she'd tease him a bit.

"They'll laugh because I'm carrying women's clothes on my head."

"So what's wrong with that, Tim?"

"You don't know what they say about that kind of thing? It mek yuh dung grow. Yuh done know dat already, mon. I don't need to have my height retarded because I carry female clothes on my head," Tim said to Essie, with a mix of Jamaican Patois dialect.

"That is ridiculous, Tim. I've never heard of that before. You are just a male chauvinist piglet who follows silly ideas."

69

In the end, Tim did help Essie with her load. He helped her all the way to the river. While at the river, Tim sat on a rock while Essie washed her clothes in the river. They talked and made fun of each other until it was time to go.

On their way back from the river, Tim helped Essie with her load, but this time they stopped to rest more often. The wet clothes, heavier now, slowed them considerably, as did the uphill journey. On one of their many rest stops, they picked some ripe mangoes off a tree. Tim climbed the tree and threw the mangoes to Essie. When they collected enough, they sat under the tree and enjoyed their treats. Refreshed, they continued on their journey home.

Essie enjoyed their time together and Tim was delighted to have spent the day with the prettiest girl in the whole town of Cascade. Tim's friendship back then when they were kids was a breath of fresh air to Essie.

Although Essie left the countryside behind, she always carried a soft spot in her heart for Tim. She'd missed her friend dearly, and sometimes wondered how he was doing. Never in her wildest dreams did she expect to see him in Montego Bay years later and of all places, at the local food market.

Therefore, in utter astonishment, she shouted to the kind vendor, "I'm Essie Streete! What's your name? Tim, right?"

"Yes, Timothy Brown," he said, nodding several times as he gazed into her eyes.

"You're Tim? My best friend, my Tim from back in Cascade?" Essie grinned, joy clear on her face.

"Essie? My sweet Essie? My Lord, I can't believe my eyes."

"Tim, what happened to you? You look so old.

They embraced, holding each other in a long and joyful hug. They rejoiced, shedding sweet tears, thrilled to see each other and to know they were both alive and well. For them, a miracle had occurred, and oblivious to those around them, Tim and Essie reconnected. They didn't care about the people staring at them as they renewed their childhood friendship.

They stepped aside as a number of years had passed between them and they had a lot to catch up on. As luck would have it, they both had kids, but they were free and single at the time. It was like it was meant to be. They did not waste any time hiding their feelings. They confessed everything to each other and initiated an intimate relationship that same day.

Essie brought Tim home to meet her kids and he spent the night at her place. After a special dinner, they spent the rest of the evening locked away in their room.

They could not have been happier with their emotional and joyful reunion. They discovered they lived in two different worlds and both liked it where they were living. However, that was not a deal breaker at all. They promised to meet each other halfway.

Tim remained in the countryside within the parish of Hanover. He lived in Clear Mount of Jericho, a small town not too far away from Cascade. He'd become an independent farmer with a large parcel of land. He brought produce to Montego Bay once a month to sell at the local market.

Essie decided not to return to the country, but vowed to maintain an intimate relationship with him long distance.

Whenever Tim was in town, he visited Essie and spent the night or a full weekend. This relationship went on for over ten years. During that time, Essie bore two sons for Tim—Karl and Leonard Brown. Leonard was four years younger than Karl.

Essie recalled a unique story about Leonard as a two-year-old. One night, Essie returned from work in a taxicab. It was late and the area where she lived had no streetlights. The headlights of the taxi provided the only light. When the cab was about two blocks away from Essie's home, there, focused in the lights, a young boy sat in the middle of the road. As the headlights approached, he started running to the side of the street, avoiding the car.

Essie saw the child and began to scream, "Stop! Stop! That's my baby! Stop! Oh my God! What on earth is he doing on the road at this time of night?" She jumped out of the car as soon as it stopped or even merely before it stopped, and ran to her son. She wondered what would have happened if she had not come home when she did. Surely her son would've been struck by a moving vehicle in the pitch dark of the night.

What had happened? Everyone was asleep, including the babysitter. Moreover, they were not aware that Leonard was able to walk so they felt he was safe in the house.

Essie quit her night job to make sure that something like that never happened again.

Years later, she remembered this horrifying incident. She often said that was when she realized her baby, Leonard, was special. From that night on, she knew in her heart he was born to be a great person and she hoped to see it happen.

Karl, on the other hand, was in safer hands. When he was two years old, Tim volunteered to keep his first baby boy with him in the country. This helped Essie with her parental load. Leonard remained with Essie and Tim supplied the family with free produce when he visited.

Chapter 13

In 1794, Robert Burns wrote:

O, my love is like a red, red rose that's newly sprung in June. O, my love is like the melody, that's sweetly played in tune. As fair thou art, my bonnie lass, so deep in love am I: and I will love thee still, my dear, till all the seas go dry: till all the seas go dry, my dear, and the rocks melt with the sun; I will love thee still my dear, while the sands of life shall run. And fare thee well, my only love, and fare thee well a while! And I will come again, my love, though it were ten thousand miles.

The long-distance relationship between Tim and Essie was blessed, wholesome, and free of major stress. Tim was madly in love with her, just as he was when a young teenager. He gave Essie his all. Anything she asked for, if it was within his means, he gave it.

The only problem was that his means were not much to a city girl. Tim's wealth was in his farmland. He had lots of it, over a hundred acres he'd gained through hard labor. Each time he reaped a crop, he used the profit to purchase more land.

The more he farmed, the more land the government gave him as incentives to increase production.

Tim was rich in real estate. The problem was no one with money would buy the land except to use for farming. Moreover, the land was not of the best quality for farming. Hard work and toil was required in order to improve the land and bring it to farmable quality. An average farmer could not afford that land, so the value of the land was low, with no potential buyers. Those lands, although valuable to Tim for his own self-worth and ability to mass produce, were worth very little for resale. Tim didn't mind that because he was happy being a farmer. He never liked having a boss anyway and he liked the peace of mind that came with living a simple, country life.

The best Tim could do for Essie was to supply her with fresh food. This was perfect for Essie because she had seven hungry mouths to feed. This made food one less thing Essie had to worry about. Her small salary took care of everything else.

Because Tim and Essie had been friends first, they understood each other's differences. One loved the country with its simple life while the other loved the big city lifestyle. They held this wholesome relationship together for almost ten years. Their ten-year relationship was the longest bond that Essie ever had. It provided her and her children the most stable period in their lives.

However, the kids were getting older. Gena, for instance, was almost an adult, approaching nineteen years old. The overall needs of Essie's family were greater than the need for food. Essie knew she could reason with Tim and that he would understand, so she went to him in the country to have a serious heart-to-heart talk. He welcomed her, treated her like a queen, and pampered her and near worshiped her. Essie didn't have to raise a hand to do anything. He cooked for her and dressed up his home when she visited. It was his pleasure to satisfy Essie in every way. He knew deep in his heart that she was in a class far above him. He believed that he was not worthy of such a beautiful sophisticated, big city lady like Essie. He was honored to have her love and attention.

So that day when Essie visited, he rolled out the red carpet. They had a wonderful dinner with their son, Karl. The meal was just the way Essie loved it. Afterwards, they sent Karl outside to play. Then they went to the bedroom and locked the door. She told him that she had something important to say to him.

"Tim, you've been my friend since I was fourteen and I want you to be my friend until the end." Then she sat down on the side of the bed beside him.

"Tim, I will always love you. You are a very special person in my life," she said softly as she leaned closer to him. "But I have something important to tell you and I would like you to understand my position."

"What is it my pretty lady? Just tell me because you know you can tell me anything. I know you more than any other person on this earth, so don't be afraid. I will understand."

"I have a lot of needs, Tim, financial needs you cannot solve. I met a wealthy guy in Montego Bay who promised to help me with my finances and I'm going to accept his offer."

Tim was silent for a long time. It was like time stood still. It seemed like the noisy silence was at least a life time long. Tim was knee-jerked by heartbreak and it hurt. His heart was severely wounded. His heart was pierced and he was bleeding heavy flow of internal sorrow. The thing he dreaded most, his biggest fear in life, had come to pass. His beloved was leaving him for a big time city guy. He felt his heart break within him, and for a moment, he forgot how to breathe as he fought the pain in his gut. He had to be strong for Essie because that's what good friends did for each other. He barely found the strength in him, but he raised his head and looked her in her eyes.

"That's okay, my love. You must do what you must to survive. I'll be right here waiting for you whenever you need me."

"Thank you, Tim, for understanding. I still love you," Essie climbed into bed with him.

They held each other close and cried because they knew it was their last time together. It was a disheartening and sad day for both of them.

Chapter 14

Bernard Dun was a self-made, wealthy, white Jamaican of short stature but large personality. He was not only short, he had a petite body structure. Handsome of face he always dressed casual.

He made his riches from livestock farming in the city. He obtained milk from his cattle and mass-produced it, thus supplying a large sector of his community. He also mass-produced eggs, beef, and poultry for commercial sale. He was well established in the town of Montego Bay, had a large, yet average-looking home on an extensive piece of property in a nice residential area of the city. His farm was at a different location from his place of residence.

Essie and Bernard created an eye-catching picture, the couple being so physically miss-matched. Essie was tall and had a thick body, while Bernard was short and thin. In spite of this, Bernard was infatuated with Essie and pursued her aggressively, offering her clothes, jewelry, money, and free livestock products.

With Tim's blessings, she welcomed Bernard's advances and from the day Essie returned to Montego Bay, she was all his. She gave herself completely to Bernard.

Bernard Dunn was a strict businessman. Therefore, he was frank and dogmatic. He made it clear to Essie that because she had so many children, they wouldn't live together, but he would wholly support her and her kids. Essie was okay with that because that was similar to how the relationship between her and Tim had been. She preferred it that way, having become used to her semi-independent lifestyle.

Essie visited Bernard on a regular basis. His visits to her home were rare. He was not a family man and although he enjoyed kids, he did not want a large family. He expressed his desire early in their relationship that he would love her to give him a child because she was such a pretty woman. He had one son of his own, but he needed another child.

That was okay with Essie. She loved her kids and believed they would change her life for the better. Every child she bore represented another chance of hope, a means of making her dreams come true. Essie dreamed of living a comfortable, worry-free life. She did not need to be rich. If riches came her way, she would not turn them down, but she only wanted the ability to give her kids a better life than she had and the hope that one day, one of them would make her proud by being a doctor, lawyer, or a great person in some noticeable manor.

Essie also did not mind having one more child if she could. She had some concerns if she still could have healthy children considering that she was now in her forties. That was her only true concern. She came to the conclusion that having babies was one of her strongest bargaining tools and she brought that belief to all of her prior relationships.

When a man saw a pretty woman like her, the first thing he thought about was having a pretty little baby of his own. It seemed like all the men in her life pursued her for her offspring.

Essie realized that God had blessed her after all, with the ability to have children; and with this ability, she was able to survive. Having kids was her survival tool, as well as her bargaining tool. So far, it seemed that she was at the losing end of all of her previous bargains, but she still had high hopes. Like an addicted gambler, she kept betting on the future prospects of her kids.

She hoped that at least one of her bargaining chips would pay off in the long run. Maybe one of her kids would turn out to be a an influential person.

It was early in their relationship when Essie became pregnant for the last time. It turned out to be a wonderful baby boy. Bernard was overjoyed and together they named the child Bunny Dun. Essie felt tremendous relief after she brought the child to full term. She was afraid that her increasingly bad habits of drinking and smoking, plus her age factor, might have prevented her from delivering a healthy baby. She also felt a big weight fall off her shoulders because she knew that her relationship with Bernard hinged on the successful delivery of a child. With Bunny, she repaid him for all the things he had done and continued to do for her and her large family.

She was nervous about the consequences of not having a successful delivery, remembering all too well how it started with the loss of her first lover, Stedman. Essie was aware that the success of her relationship hinged on her ability to produce a healthy baby.

They maintained their arrangement until Bunny grew older. As Bunny aged, Bernard cut back on the support payments and eventually told Essie he was unable to support her family and could only give just enough child support for Bunny.

He even started decreasing the amount of support for Bunny. Essie was hit with hypocritical and deceitful rejection. Essie was upset but not at all surprised. She saw it coming and knew all along that Bernard was only nice to her because he badly wanted a child from her and would do anything to get one. She was right about him all along.

Essie felt better when she considered it was not a bad deal. He had something she needed and she had something he needed, and it had been a good arrangement while it lasted. Now she had to do what she did best-- lean on her single parent strength and skills to make it.

Essie did not complain. She braced herself to find a job as a chef so she could stay in the two-bedroom apartment that Conroy Levy initially had gotten for her.

Chapter 15

Essie went back to work at a large, ten-bedroom private resort in Iron Sure, owned by Dr. McNelly. He was a rich, white American, a snowbird, who decided to purchase the large home as a vacation retreat. When he was not in residence, it doubled as a guesthouse. He lived in the United States and visited Jamaica once or twice a year during the winter months.

Dr. McNelly hired a local real estate company to manage and maintain the residence. They functioned as a travel agency and residential management group, placing advertisements around the world for tourists to lease the mansion. The company hired staff to take care of the property, including a chambermaid, a butler, who was also a gardener, and Essie as the chef.

Essie was excited. She'd prayed for this type of work. No disgruntled manager peered over her shoulders or questioned her recipes. She was her own boss as long as the guests did not complain about her service or her cooking. She felt confident And knew that this was a place where she would be able to take her natural skill in cooking to the next level. She began an intense reading and self-education program at the Montego Bay Public Library every chance she got.

While returning from the library one day, Essie met an interesting man named Ruben Malcolm. He was a little older than her but very handsome and well built, with a muscular body. He approached Essie and asked if she would like to go out with him, stating he was single with no kids. He had just separated from his wife, but neglected to tell Essie that. She liked him and, even with as many bad experiences with men as she'd already endured, she needed a strong man to lean on. However, this time, Essie was firm about what she wanted in the relationship. After many failure relationships, she knew what she wanted and what she didn't.

"Ruben, I have eight kids and I don't intend to have anymore."

"Well, lovely lady, you don't have to worry about that. I'm comfortable without my own children. Your kids will be mine. I always dreamed of being a part of a large family, even if it wasn't mine."

"I have six kids living with me so I don't want any overnights. You can visit, but you can't stay. I don't mind meeting at your place or anywhere else you want me to meet you."

"Yes, that will be fine with me," Ruben replied.

"I have financial commitments I will need your help with. If you don't have any money, I don't want to waste my time. Okay, Ruben? We need to establish these things from the start."

"I work a construction job. I have a lot of money when work is good and I have very little when it gets scarce."

"Okay, then as long as we have everything clear, we can date each other and see where it goes."

"Okay, let's start by having dinner somewhere nice. Is that a deal?"

"Deal," Essie replied.

That was the start of Essie's relationship with Ruben. Essie felt proud of herself. It felt good to demand what she wanted. She wished she had that strength in the earlier part of her life. Maybe her life would have been different. After all, life was just a matter of deals and breaks. Essie and Ruben had a long, wonderful relationship. It was a complete reversal from Essie's former experience with men.

Ruben kept on trying to get closer to Essie and her family. Essie was the one holding him back. He wanted to be a part of her family. He wanted to be a real father to her kids. When he was around them, the pride he felt showed in his face. He made himself useful when he visited Essie's apartment. He fixed everything that was broken and tried to play a fatherly role to each child.

Ruben believed that kids and a family, in general, needed more than money. He believed they needed fatherly love and attention, usually missing in a single female family. He believed that with fatherly love and personal attention, kids could go far in life because it gave them the confidence a mother alone could not instill.

He believed that the psychological development of children required 50/50 input by both parents. A single mother, with her best efforts, could only improve her input by up to sixty percent at best. Therefore, Ruben believed that the children of single parents were never fully balanced or developed to their maximum potential, no matter

84

how much time and money one of their parents gave them.

In Ruben's opinion, kids need both parents equally and they should only be denied that basic need if there was no other viable alternative. Moreover, this was Ruben's chance to feel what it would be like if he had kids and a large family of his own.

Essie didn't want him to change the structure or dynamics of her family. Her kids were mostly grown and she couldn't risk putting a father in their lives just to see him walk away, leaving them brokenhearted. She wanted to shield them from that disaster by taking the full brunt of the blow by herself. She considered herself an expert in being brokenhearted. she could deal with it, but not her kids.

Therefore, she never gave Ruben the chance to fill a fatherly role in her family. Skeptical, she kept him at a distance and would call him only when she needed him or when she visited him. Essie never let him into their lives.

That arrangement worked well until one day while she relaxed in his bed, a seemingly mad woman broke into the house and tried fighting her. Essie had to run for her life.

Once more, fear struck her and she abandoned her relationship with Ruben when she found out the mad woman was his ex-wife. She landed on her feet, started running, and never looked back.

Chapter 16

The horn of the country bus bellowed as it ripped around the corner. Its front looked old and overworked as it approached. Grayish-black smoke streamed into the air from its tail and the bus leaned to one side as if it was about to roll over.

Essie had taken her kids to the countryside to spend a few summer days near Tim. They loved it and looked forward to the annual trip. This time, they had gone by way of bus.

It was overloaded with baskets and bags full of fruits, green bananas, potatoes, and other produce from the countryside. There was no space left on top of the bus, not even enough for a fly.

The square-faced, rusty, red and grey caravan pulled up to the bus stop at Jericho Square. Still leaning to one side, it jolted and bucked twice before it came to a complete stop. It sank lower to the ground as it stopped.

The frisky bus conductor, dressed in a full suit of brown shirt and pants, was swinging from the door aiming to jump out of the bus long before it came to a stop. By the time the vehicle stopped, he was already on the side of the road jogging alongside it. And soon, he was at the back climbing on top of the bus, getting ready to unload the needed items.

The passengers poured out of the two doorless doorways in an orderly manner. An elderly lady stepped off the bus through the front exit and was followed by a continuous line of passengers.

At the back door, fourteen-year-old Junior leaped out of the bus. "Jericho, we are here!" he shouted.

Gena, age sixteen, sprang out right behind him. "Yeah, we are here," she said. "Come, guys, let's go to the back of the bus to get our stuff." Happy and excited to have reached her destination, she held out her hand to Betty to help her down the steps.

"Thank you, Gena," thirteen-year-old Betty said.

"You're welcome, Betty." Gena turned to help Myrtle, who was eleven. Gena reached for Myrtle's hand and guided her safely out of the doorway.

"Thank yuh, Sis," Myrtle accepted Gena's helping hands.

"Everybody move out the way. I'm going to jump!" Leonard, age six, yelled.

"No! You might fall! Don't do it!" Gena shouted.

"I won't. I will be okay. Look!" Leonard leaped out of the back door of the bus and landed safely on his feet, though off balance.

"See, I told you I could do it."

"That was a lucky jump. You almost fell," Gena said with a frown upon her face.

"Yes, but I did not. That's what matters, right?"

"Whatever," Gena responded. "Let's head to the back with Junior to get our stuff."

"Where are Momma and Bunny?" Myrtle asked.

"They are at the front of the bus. They'll be out soon," Gena said to her little sister. No sooner had the words left Gena's mouth, than Essie stepped out of the front door. She was holding two-year-old Bunny in her hands.

"Guys, did you get our bags?" Essie asked.

"Not yet, Momma," Gena said as the kids all rushed to the back of the bus. Junior was in position to catch the first bag, which the bus conductor was about to throw down.

"Boy, can you catch?" the conductor asked Junior. He was bravely standing on top of the mountainous load of luggage between large baskets, bags, and pans. Before Junior could say a word, the bag was on its way down.

"Yes, I ca...haw! Got it!" Junior caught the bag. He passed it to Gena who placed it carefully on the roadside beside a wall.

"Next one! I'm ready," said Junior and he continued to receive their luggage until he had four bags and two suitcases.

They gathered their belongings and headed to the hills of Clear Mount. Essie led the way. Gena was now holding baby Bunny. The town of Clear Mount was in sight. "There it is!" Leonard shouted. "We're almost there."

"Yes, I can see the big mango tree. There goes Mast Tim's gateway!" Myrtle screamed. She took off running. She ran toward the town's narrow entrance. Leonard followed behind her. They raced ahead to see who would be the first to get there.

"I bet I can beat you both to the mango tree!" Junior shouted. He waited until Myrtle and Leonard were far enough ahead and then took off running. Betty also followed. The kids raced ahead, leaving Essie and Gena behind.

"Be careful, guys. If you keep on running like that, you might fall!" Essie called out to her kids, but they were too excited to hear or even care to listen to her.

Junior ripped past them and was the first to get to the familiar mango tree. By the time they all got there, they were out of breath. They were panting and gasping for air as they sat on the root of the tree. The big, thick, solid roots were three to four feet above the ground. The children rested while they waited for their mom, Gena, and baby Bunny to arrive.

In no time, there was a handful of curious country kids standing along the street in front of the gateway. They stood on the street watching the bunch of town folks enter their village. Ten-year-old Karl heard the noise outside his gate. He ran to the door to see what was going on. He ran out the door yelling, "Momma! Momma! You are here!" Karl rushed into his mother's open arms. He was happy to see her and all of his brothers and sisters. He greeted all of them as well.

"Hello, Karl. How are you, son?" Essie said, and she stooped down to his level, hugged him, and kissed him on the cheek.

"I'm fine, Momma."

"Is your dad home?"

"Yes, Momma. He is cooking in the kitchen."

After they greeted each other, they went down to Tim's house to greet him. Before long, the kids were back outside playing with Karl and his friends. They played until suppertime. After they ate, Essie instructed the kids to take a bath and change into some clean clothes before night fell.

While the kids took their baths, they ran short on water. The water drums were critically low. Karl volunteered to rush to the public water pipe to refill the drums with water so they could finish bathing and prepare for the evening's activities. That night's scheduled activity was what they called "story time by Essie."

Karl made many trips back and forth to the public water pipe. On his last trip, he stopped to pitch a game of marbles with some friends, whom he had met up with at the pipe area. He was also engaged in a game called stone tag. This was a game in which they would take turns tossing a particular chosen stone at each other's stones. The first one to hit their opponent's target stone was the winner. Karl lost track of time.

By the time he realized this, it was already late into the evening. It was getting dark. "Oh my God! It's getting late. I must go before night falls," Karl said to his friends. He bid them good-bye and ran off to fetch his last bucket of water.

On his way home, he had a strange encounter. He was walking with the bucket of water on his head. It had just turned from dusk to dark. He was being led along his pathway by the glowing light of the moon. After he approached the straight, narrow, open stretch of dirt road leading to his home, he realized that he was the only person on the streets.

It seemed like he was the only person in the entire village out at that time. All activities in the country town of Clear Mount stopped at six o'clock. The village seemed to be asleep by seven thirty. It was now eight, give or take a few minutes.

He had just made it around a deep corner of the undeveloped road when he started up a steep curve. Suddenly, a tingling chill blanketed his entire body. Karl's heart skipped a beat or two. His head felt like it was growing larger and larger. It felt like it was growing out of proportion to his body. In the distance, he saw an image bearing the likeness of an animal. However, this was no ordinary animal. It appeared to be a giant cow or ox. It appeared to be coming at full speed toward him. It had an iron chain tied around its neck. The iron chain was long. Most of it was being dragged behind the beast as it raced toward him.

He was shocked and afraid. His eyes were flooded with panic. His palms were sweating. His whole body was shivering with fear. He took off running back in the opposite direction. When he looked back, he saw that the creature was catching up to him and he realized that he still had the bucket of water on his head. Of course, he then threw it away so quickly, one would think that he had been hit by an electric shock wave. He also realized that he had hit his right big toe on a stone while running. It was bleeding significantly. He was running and hopping as he tried to make his getaway.

He glanced back to see how he was doing. To his surprise, the angry beast was closing in on him. It was so close Karl could smell its rotten, rancid breath. He could also clearly see the strange look in the beast's eyes. Its head was enormous and it had large, bulging eyes. Karl thought it was strange that the beast's eyes were as red as fire, but resembled human eyes.

Karl realized that this gigantic creature was not an animal. No, it definitely was not. It was what they, in the countryside of Hanover, referred to as a "rolling calf." Yes! Karl was being chased by a ghost! He was frightened, completely terrified. His head felt, larger than his body and was growing bigger yet. His feet felt weak and his knees shook like an unbalanced washing machine. His whole body was wobbly and uncoordinated, because he was shaking uncontrollably with fear.

He had heard stories about various rolling calf encounters, but he had never seen one before—well, at least not until now. A rolling calf was a ghost that appeared in the form of an animal. Most people who had close encounters reported that they first heard or detected the rolling calves by their unique, loud, and unnerving clanking noise. This sound was made by the long chain that they dragged behind them. They had large, red eyes like a dragon. Some said that the beasts could breathe fire through their mouths.

Some people said that rolling calves were the spirits of evil butchers who had been cruel when they were alive. The best way to get away from the monstrous beasts was to drop items on the ground. The rolling calves would have to stop to count each items. Reports of past encounters indicated that this getaway method worked every time.

Karl started running, like he hadn't run before. He forgot about his damaged toe. He was going at top speed, like Carl Lewis or Asafa Powell. He was all-out straight sprinting. He shifted into sixth gear and took off blazing the trail for his dear life. Neither Usain Bolt nor Michael Johnson could have kept up with Karl that night. He was sure that he must have broken some kind of world record. He was on the verge of flying, as he could feel the wind rushing by him like a turbulent storm.

A strange thought came to him while running for his life. He heard a voice inside his head repeating, "Boy, this country place is no place for a coward like you. Why are you here running for your dear life when your family is living nicely and comfortably in the big city of Montego Bay? Boy you've been grossly neglected and discarded into these bushes, and that's just not right. That's just not right."

He didn't remember how he got home that night, but he had lived to tell the tale. However, from that night on, he disliked the countryside of Clear Mount. He would rather do anything or live anywhere than continue living a backward, country lifestyle. Karl decided that he wanted to live with his brothers and sisters.

He made it home to tell his brothers and sisters about his frightening story. "Leonard, Myrtle, everybody, you'll never imagine what just happened to me." Karl burst through the doorway and into the living room. He looked frightened and was breathing heavily.

"Oh Lord! Karl, what happened to you? You look like you've seen a ghost or something!"

93

Essie cried. The rest of the kids dashed to the living room to see what the big commotion was.

"I did, Momma. I did." Karl sank into the couch. He was trying to catch his breath.

"Boy, don't be ridiculous. There is no such thing as a ghost," she said. "You must have seen a shadow or something."

"No, Momma, I did. I saw a…I saw a…I saw a rolling calf!" Karl belted out, now in tears. "I saw a rolling calf. It…it…it chased me all the way home."

"Karl, did…did you…you…you say <u>rolling calf</u>?" Betty asked, shaking with fear.

"Yes, it chased me all the…the…the way home!"

"I'm never going outside at night, never ever," said Leonard. He was also trembling. His eyes bulged with hysteria. The kids were nervous and scared that night.

"Calm down, guys. Calm down. Rolling calves are not real. They do not exist. There is nothing to fear. Karl must have seen an animal that was loose and was out of control on the streets." Essie was able to calm her kids down that night; but from that day on, Karl was never the same.

Chapter 17

At forty-five, Essie was a wiser and stronger person than she had been when she was younger. She knew exactly what she wanted out of life. She was determined not to let herself be pushed around by any man again. She was tired of being used and disregarded by men. She was determined to put a stop to all of the provocative abuse in her life. Essie realized that nothing in life came easily. Therefore, her love and her attention would not be easily obtained either. All her love and attention would be for her kids and her kids only. If any man wanted it, he would have to be willing to sacrifice a lot.

This was the attitude she had toward Dr. McNelly When Dr. McNelly visited his cottage without his wife, it was unusual because during his previous visits, he brought with him his wife and kids. This time he came alone with plans to spend three months there. He was sixty-three years old and had just retired.

Essie was one of his favorite staff members. He praised her each day after he finished eating her cooking. The sensational aromas of her tantalizing meals stimulated his appetite. He anticipated her island-style foods.

He loved her cooking. One day, after enjoying a scrumptious lunch, he came into the kitchen to praise her for her outstanding cooking, as he usually did.

The sweet-smelling aroma of the island spices hung in the air. It filled his nostrils and titillated his appetite all over again. His appetite drove him mad for something more than food. It must have been the horny goat weed that she skillfully added to the aphrodisiacal clam preparation. Maybe it was the soul-soothing Cajun sauce or the jerk island spices that she used to sauté the lobster for lunch, or maybe it was the teasing amount of caviar that she sprinkled over his meal as a topping. Whatever it was, it was working its magic.

He complimented her as usual. However, this time, he embraced her softly with his hands resting on her buttocks. They hugged for a long time, and then he kissed her on her cheek. She recognized what her boss was trying to do, and she was not about to let this opportunity pass her by. She thought to herself, *This man is a very, very rich man.* Maybe this was her ticket to travel to the United States or an opportunity to get a raise or a large sum of money. She decided not to deny him anything. Therefore, while still in his embrace, Essie made a seductive gesture. She turned her head and looked up into his wanting eyes, and then she smiled. Dr. McNelly was pleased to see her reaction. They basked in the sweet, tantalizing aroma lingering in the air.

This passionate occasion set the stage for more between Essie and her boss. The lovers were discreet about their affair. They met after the other two employees left for the day. It was part of the chef's job to stay overnight at the cottage. The other two employees, the chambermaid and the gardener, worked standard hours, from nine to five. Therefore, the situation was favorable for Dr. McNelly and Essie.

After about six weeks of the affair, Essie decided that it was time to have a serious talk with Dr. McNelly. He had two weeks remaining before he left the island. Essie timed him carefully on their next sexual encounter. After he went into his room, she slipped in behind him and closed the door. She swiftly changed into provocative, red, seductive lingerie. She enticingly paraded around the room like a Victoria's Secret model.

He beckoned her to come closer, but she did not. She continued to flirtatiously model her outfit around the room. Discerning his state, Essie said to him, "Doc, you know that I have eight kids to take care of, and I'm both their father and their mother? Did you know that they all live in one bedroom?"

"How can I help, Essie? Just let me know."

"Doc, my kids are all getting big. I need a decent home for them."

"How much is a nice, three-bedroom house going for in Jamaica?"

"I don't know, Doc, but I can find out."

"Okay, Essie Do that. Look around and let me know. I will take care of you if you take care of me," the retired doctor replied.

"Thank you, Doc." She jumped into bed with him. The next day was Essie's day off. She did not waste any time getting started on her house-hunting project. She went to the district of Glenworth because she had once overheard rumors that some wonderful houses were for sale there and that it was a fast-growing neighborhood where one could get the most for one's money. She met a man by the name of Mr. Gibbs, who was selling a spiffy, three-bedroom, single-family house. It a nice front patio overlooking the cul-de-sac of a street nearby. The house was made of wood, as opposed to building blocks.

Essie thought that she had a better chance of affording this home. Moreover, it was in an excellent location where one could see the ocean out in the distance. You could also see the wonderful sunrise in the mornings from the front porch. She asked Mr. Gibbs for the price of the house, and he told her that the house was underpriced to sell expeditiously. The house was being sold for only fifty-five thousand U.S. dollars.

The next day at work, Essie told Dr. McNelly the price of the house, and he reached for his checkbook and wrote a check for twenty-five thousand dollars. Essie was grateful but befuddled because she was not sure if Dr. McNelly had understood the price she quoted him. She repeated the price. Dr McNelly replied, "Essie, you may take the day off today. Tomorrow, you can come by for the remaining amount." Essie was even more bewildered.

After all was said and done, she received a huge check. This was the lump sum that she had fantasized about. It was sobering when it dawned on her that her boss had handed her the unbelievable amount of fifty-five thousand U.S. dollars. This was better than hitting the jackpot. This didn't happen in an average person's life. Essie

realized that this one fortune made up for all of the
other misfortunes in her life.

Chapter 18

The girls had one room, the boys had another room, and Essie, the hardworking queen of the family, had her own room as well. It was like an instant change in social class and status. The family felt revived and rescued from the gripping claws of the ghetto. Now they could hold their heads up high with pride and dream big dreams. Owning their own home, free of any mortgage or rent, was a tremendous boost to everyone's confidence.

Essie was happy for the change in her family's lifestyle. She was proud of their new home. However, over time, she developed problems sleeping at night, so she started doubling her alcohol intake. Her smoking habit, which she had once tried to quit, was now worse. Essie had become a fighter in the battle of her own struggle to survive. She knew that she had to keep on fighting because her children needed her more than ever.

She received another offer from a similar private cottage in the same area of Iron Shore, and she was contemplating accepting the new job. They had offered her a much higher salary because they had heard of her excellent cooking skills. It was a standing offer. In an attempt to steal her away from her job, the new company had given her this higher offer over a year earlier. Essie didn't accept it at the time because of her loyalty to her current boss. She believed that with the fringe benefits, her job was worth more than what the other company was offering in the long run. But when they called again and raised the offer higher than before, it was easy for Essie to leave her current job.

Essie was serious about life now, and she wasn't going to take any second-best job. She knew that she was a first-class chef, and she wasn't going to settle for less. She had a family to feed and clothe, and therefore, she drove a hard bargain.

Essie worked hard while her family developed their own individual identities. Now that the family was settled in their home, Karl separated voluntarily from his father Mr. Timothy Brown, to join the family in Glenworth. He was fourteen years old and was fed up with the country lifestyle. Karl completed his secondary education at Glenworth All-Age School and went on to a trade school to study welding.

At twenty-one years old, Gena, the miracle baby, was a mother of three boys: Don, Andre, and Breath. Don was the oldest of the three boys and prior to this time, had been living mostly with his father's family. Breath was the youngest and was clingy to his grandmother, Essie. Andre fell in the middle; he was the quietest of the boys.

Gena got her big break when she got a visa to go to Nassau, Bahamas. The day she left, she trustingly left her kids with their grandmother, Essie. She cried and vowed that she was going to make it and pave the way for her family to follow.

Gena quickly obtained a job in the Bahamas and started sending food and clothes for the family every major holiday. Within two years, Gena, to everyone's surprise, made a call to her family to let them know that she had made it safely to the United States. She had made it through a risky stowaway mission on a major cruise ship. It was not an easy journey. She had been abused by multiple crew members and was almost thrown overboard.

She persevered and lived to tell the story. She didn't tell her family about the gruesome parts of her journey. She only told them about the good news concerning her successful arrival at the United States.

For many years, she struggled to survive in New York City, but she found a way to continue her regular support to the family. Gena had a special closet that she reserved for her family's stuff. After she filled and sent off a minimum of two barrels with one containing food and the other containing clothes, shoes, and other stuff, she would start on the preparation of the next package.

Each time she went to the supermarket or to do some type of shopping, she searched for the two-for-one deals or any incredible deals in general.

She bought these items with certain family members' names in mind. When she got home, she sorted her newly bought items. She meticulously put a name on each piece of clothing or pair of shoes.

She also sometimes wrote little notes concerning each item, such as "for Bunny's birthday," and she pinned them to the items. She would then carefully store them away in her reserved closet. She would put food items directly into the food barrel. She continued this process until both barrels were full or it was the next holiday and time to call the international freight carrier.

Holidays for Essie's family meant that barrels were on the way from the United States. There was always a level of excitement in the air. They held their breath with anticipation. They never knew what was going to be in the barrel for them. However, one thing was for sure: there was something in the barrel for everyone. Whether it fit was a different story, but Gena never forgot or omitted anyone.

Once the barrels arrived, the holiday officially began. The family members were as anxious as children at Christmas who had received their wrapped gifts and couldn't wait to rip into them to see what Santa had left for them. Usually, the food barrel didn't draw much attention. It was the barrel of stuff that magnetically drew the crowd of Essie's family around it. Once the cover of the barrel was removed, everyone would rush in to see what was in the barrel for him or her.

The male members of the family went for the clothes or male-related stuff, and the females, likewise, dove into the barrel to pull out female-related stuff. They checked to see if their names were written on the items. As a name was identified, that person would dash forward to joyously collect his or her item. Sometimes, the barrel ceremony was more organized.

At times, there was a designated leader or distributor. This distributor was responsible for opening the barrel and picking up the items one by one. However, it was hard to find a good distributor, because there was so much excitement in the air that once the distributor started and ran into his or her own name, he or she stopped to admire or try on the new item.

As might be expected, no one was willing to wait around on such time-wasting activities or gestures. It led right back to the pandemonium and individual diving and scooping up of items in no semblance of order. It was like Christmas morning on each holiday, and Gena was like the Santa Claus of the family.

The excitement did not end with the distribution of the gifts. After each person collected his or her share of goods, it was time to try them on and hope that they were the right size. Gena had a unique skill of detecting the changing sizes of each member of her family. It was rare for an item not to fit.

However, when that did happen, there was more pandemonium as trade-offs occurred among the family. It sometimes appeared like the scene in the story of Cinderella where the stepsisters forced their too-big feet into the tiny slipper trying to fit into the tiny glass slipper brought by the prince.

After the opening of the barrel, or what was humorously perceived as the opening ceremony and, there was the trade show. Everyone tried on their clothes and shoes to see if they fit and to see what they could profitably trade for another item. Sometimes, the trade was not only based on fit but also on preferences.

Once everyone obtained the appropriate items, the next step was the display show. This was the best part of the whole barrel activity. Everyone wanted to wear their new clothes or shoes. There was always an occasion or reason to utilize these new things. It was obvious to the community when the barrel had been received by Essie's family because everyone would be out roaming the streets in their new apparel thanking God for Essie's miracle baby, Gena.

At ten years of age, Leonard vowed to become a doctor one day, so he could help the family while healing the world. Everyone in his family laughed at him and called him funny names because he was the goofy and nerdy kid in the bunch. They called him "the Reverence," which was the shortened form of an even longer, more ridiculous nickname: "Leonard the Reverence-Ripe-Banana-Junjay." He knew there was a story behind that name, but he never figured out what it meant. He believed it was a form of mockery to indicate that he was a fool.

They were right. Considering the odds stacked against him, he was a fool to think that he could make it to the top of the intellectual hierarchy to become a physician, especially coming from the bottom with no support structure.

Leonard didn't care how impossible it seemed. He did not mind if they laughed at him. He was determined to become a doctor. He wanted to contribute to society. He wanted to help his struggling family, and in a big way. He got baptized in the Seventh-Day Adventist (SDA) Church at the age of ten. Shortly after Myrtle stopped attending.

Myrtle attended the SDA church since being invited by a neighbor, Mr. Mulgrave. She was baptized one year later. She attended church every Sabbath and had almost perfect attendance. She was the only member of Essie's family who followed a religious pathway.

However, Myrtle quit after discovering she had rheumatic fever and heart disease. She also quit school and started roaming the acting rebellious. She fought, drank alcohol, and smoked marijuana. She also got pregnant, against her doctor's advice. She gave birth to a baby, named Dean Myers seven months into her pregnancy.

Junior, at age nineteen, also smoked marijuana. He was an apprentice to an electrician. He later became a popular electrician in his community. Junior had a baby girl, Denise, with a woman named Pauline.

Betty was the prettiest child of all Essie's children. She was heavyset, but had a pretty face. At eighteen, she decided to become a beautician after trying her hand at dressmaking. She went on to own a beauty parlor. She gave birth to twin girls, Kate and Keisha. She later had another girl named Charlene.

Lela, who lived with Miriam, went to an exclusive SDA private school. She wanted to be a nurse.

Bunny, the most handsome boy in the family, was young and undecided as to what he wanted to be. He was very charming and had a way with words. He was an outstanding speaker. The family envisioned him becoming a politician someday.

Chapter 19

Essie had an awe-inspiring, unusual, and noteworthy habit. When she went to town to shop, she always spotted young girls who needed help or shelter. It was like she had developed an eye or skill for that particular situation. When she spotted the young lady in need, she walked over and asked them if needed help. The young ladies readily reveal their stories to her.

Sometimes, a girl needed taxi fare. Other times, a girl was lost and needed directions. Most often, however, a girl was a runaway teenager looking for a place to stay. Essie was skillful in spotting the girls amid of a crowded plaza. While the average person did not notice anything strange about the girls, Essie did. It didn't matter how busy she was, she identified and approach them. She astutely figured out what it was they needed and gave it to them from her own resources.

If she was not able to help them herself, she stayed with them until they were helped. Many times, they stayed the night, or longer if necessary, so reached their destination or reached their target person. When the girl was a runaway, she would take her into her home and have her do light chores for pay. She did this for the women so they would be able to save money, obtain a job, get an education, or meet a partner in order to move on and live an independent life.

Essie's home sometimes appeared was like a rehabilitation center. There could be as few as one per year or as many as six in the same month. There were no age restrictions either. A lady at age thirty-nine could need rescue from an abusive husband. Essie was brilliant at noticing a person in need of help.

Among the women that Essie took in was Pauline Anderson. Pauline was a runaway from the town of May Pen in the parish of Clarendon. She had a tattered shopping bag in her hand with what seemed to be a few groceries in it. Essie was in town shopping at the same plaza. She noticed something strange about the young lady as the girl pretentiously walked around as if she was involved in the same shopping activities as the rest of the crowd of shoppers. Essie noticed that the teenager was not buying anything. She was staring despondently into people's faces rather than looking at grocery items. The girl had a familiar destitute look in her eyes.

Essie knew that she had to be a runaway teen. She walked up to the young lady and asked her if she could be of some help. "Hello, young lady, what is your name? May I help you with anything today?" As Essie inquired about her needs, the girl looked up at her with a bewildered look.

"No, ma'am, I am just shopping," she replied very confidently; but for a split second, a sign of irritation or displeasure crossed her face as if she was in no mood to deal with a stranger.

"What's in your bag?" Essie asked.

Not any business of yours, the girl thought. But instead, she said, "Just some groceries," with an annoyed frown upon her face.

"Are you sure I can't help you with anything?" Essie asked one more time.

"Do I look like someone who needs help?" the young lady said, aggravated.

Essie answered assertively, "Yes, you do, and this is a cold, mean place for you to take any chances with your life. Go home to your parents; you will be better off." Shocked, the young lady stared into Essie's eyes and saw the deep, unusual motherly concern in her face.

The young lady shouted, "I'm looking for a nice, single man to take me home. Why do you care anyway?"

"I care because I've been there before, and I know that things don't always work out the way you intend."

"I just got here from May Pen, and I don't intend to go back. I want to start a life for myself."

"I can see that you just got here. Kids are usually confident in the morning, much more than they are in the evening. What is your name, young lady?"

"My name is Pauline, miss."

"Well, Pauline, my name is Miss Essie. I must tell you the truth; you don't need a man. What you need is a job. I'm not rich. I can hardly take care of my large family at home, but they have a roof over their heads, and it's all mine. You can join my family and help with the cooking and cleaning when I'm away, and I will give you a small salary.

When you are ready, you can get a decent job and help yourself."

"Thank you, Miss Essie."

After shopping together, they went home. When Essie introduced her to her family, no one was surprised. Everyone welcomed Pauline with open arms, like she was another sibling who had been added to their family. Pauline was amazed to see how friendly and accepting everyone was to her. She noticed that the family did not have many fancy things, but the house was clean and the family was a happy and peaceful one—well, except for Myrtle. Every now and then, she got into a fight at her school.

Pauline was shy at first, but as time went on, she became more comfortable and started opening up and gave them the full story of her background. She said that her parents were too strict and she did not like the town of May Pen. Therefore, being curious, she wanted to know what life was like in a bigger city like Montego Bay.

Essie decided to research Pauline's background and she found out that her parents were decent parents. The problem was that they pushed Pauline too hard to get the best out of her life, which was what subsequently drove her away. They meant well, and they really loved and missed her. When Essie first contacted Pauline's parents, they were happy to know that she was alive and doing well and was in good hands.

They made plans to meet Pauline at Essie's house. When they finally saw her, Pauline's whole family shed tears of joy to see how happy, neat, and clean she looked. They decided to respect Pauline's wishes to remain with Essie's family.

Essie's children were now teenagers or older, but Essie was still the main breadwinner of the family. This was tested when she was in a terrible car accident one night while coming home from work. There were five passengers in the taxi when the car ran t out of control and hit another vehicle. The taxi was destroyed and everyone was injured, but thank goodness, no one died that night.

Essie's upper teeth were knocked out of her mouth. She had other injuries, but nothing major. That night, Essie's family realized that they could not afford to lose their only parent figure. They cried frantically for Essie when they first heard the news of the accident. They cried because they loved her, but also because they realized she was all they had. They could not live without her.

That accident was a wake-up call to all of her kids, who had believed that Essie was immortal and would always be there.

Essie recovered, and her kids learned a lesson: do not take her for granted. They told her every day that they loved her and appreciated her.

Essie also had a wake-up call from that accident. She realized that she needed to take better care of her body and stop smoking and drinking. She made many attempts after that accident to stop smoking, but she failed each time.

Chapter 20

"Happy birthday, Junior, no Karl... hmm..."

"Bunny, Momma, I'm Bunny."

"Yes, Bunny, I meant to say Bunny. Today is your birthday."

"I know, Momma," he said, with a look that indicated he couldn't forget it if he tried.

Unlike other nurturing parents, with the exception of a family beach day on one particular Easter holiday, Essie didn't take her family to the movies or to family gatherings. They spent no time on family trips or weekend vacations. She was too busy working to put food on the table and provide other basics. She was sometimes even too busy to celebrate the kids' birthdays.

"Happy birthday, son. Today you're seven years old."

"I know, Momma," Bunny said as if it was no big deal.

"Come give your mother a big hug." Essie held out her arms. He ran to her as if he could be in for a big surprise.

"Junior, ah," she struggled again to remember his name.

"Bunny, Momma," he said. He knew she loved him but sometimes got too busy and confused to remember his name, even after seven years of being a member in his large family. Sometimes, it took her several attempts to get it right. She usually used the wrong names, starting with the oldest child, the most familiar, and then traveled down the line until she got to the right name. It was not a major problem for them.

The children were familiar with her shortcomings and did their best to help by identifying themselves when they sensed her confusion.

"Yes, Bunny, may you live to see many more birthdays. May you grow up to be a fine young man and have a wonderful life and remember your mother when she's old and gray. Okay, son?" Essie picked him up, held him inches from her face, and gave him a big kiss on his cheek.

"Thank you, Momma," he said as she put him back on the floor.

"So sorry I'm not rich. I wish I could give you everything you want, but at least I'll make sure that you don't starve and you always have a roof over your head. Okay, son?"

"Okay, Momma. No problem. So I'm not getting anything for my birthday today?" He tried to understand the mombo jombo confusing stuff his mother said.

"Bunny, don't you remember? Gena sent you your birthday gift at Christmas. Remember, the sneakers she sent you had a written note that said, 'For Bunny's birthday'? Do you remember?"

"Oh, yes. I forgot about my sneakers. Gena always remembers my birthday," he said, as if no one else did.

"Oh, may God bless her. She is my lovely God blessed miracle baby. I don't know what I would've done without her. She raised her hands toward the heavens. —Thank you, Father, for my daughter, Gena."

"Wow! Gena sent me my birthday gift three months early. That was why I forgot, Momma. That was why I forgot."

"Bunny, I'll also bake a cake at work for you. I'll bring it down to you on Friday, okay?"

"Okay, Momma, thank you. I love you. I love Gena too."

"We love you too, my son."

"Momma, when is Gena coming back to Jamaica?"

"I don't know. I don't know. Maybe you should write her a letter and ask her. You know how she loves to hear from you kids, so write her a letter and I'll post it."

"I'm going to write her a letter today."

"That's good. I've to get to work now and I'm running late. You know what a long walk it is."

"Momma, why don't yuh take a cab to work today?" Myrtle asked Essie.

Myrtle had been sitting on the front porch steps listening to the conversation. She sat observing the sky and the wonderful morning sunrise as the sun rose above the serene ocean lining way out in the distant view. "Yuh don't have to walk in the burning sun every day, Momma, yuh know that, right?"

"My dear child, I don't have enough money to take a taxi to work. I have to leave money for you all to have lunch and dinner. But sometimes I get lucky and a car stops for me and gives me a lift to the bus stop. I hope I get lucky today because I'm tired of walking, especially in the blazing hot sun, and in addition to that, when I reach Half Moon, I've to walk over that long hillside to get to work. Oh Lord I get so tired sometimes," Essie complained, her voice low.

"Madda, are you coming back home this evening or are you staying at work all week?" Karl asked.

"Yes, I'm coming home tonight. I usually only stay overnight if I have a guest; but there're no guests, so I'll be back tonight. I might be a little late, but Betty will cook dinner, so don't worry."

He snorted rudely. —I'm not worried. I never get worried. I'm a country man and I eat anything that moves. I know how to survive. Don't you worry about me; worry about yourself," he said, voice boorish and impolite.

"Karl, why are you always so nasty? You should know by now how to talk to me. I'm your mother. You know that."

Karl walked toward the room he shared with Junior, Leonard, Bunny, Andre, Breath, and Don.

Betty, Pauline, and Myrtle, plus Essie's latest additions to the family, Paulette and Pauline, twin sisters seeking refuge from the street, shared the other bedroom. Since there was already a Pauline in the family, they referred to the other Pauline as "Pauline the twin."

Pauline the twin and Paulette joined the family after Essie went to buy meat from the butcher shop. She spotted the two young ladies, who were about eighteen, sitting on the same wall downtown where she'd sat twenty years earlier. That's where she had met Gena's father, Rev.

115

Murray. The two ladies looked worried, but Essie wasn't sure what to make of them until she was on her way back home. She noticed them still sitting there. The only difference was that one of them was in tears while the other offered comfort. Essie was sure they needed help, so she went over to introduce herself.

"Hello, young ladies, I'm Miss Essie. I noticed you're both looking sad today. What is the problem?"

"We're fine, miss. Thank you," Pauline the twin said.

"Then why is your sister crying? Why don't you take her home if she is not feeling well?" No sooner had the words left Essie's mouth, when Paulette burst into tears.

"No! We're not okay, miss. We're not okay at all. She's lying."

"What is the problem?"

"I shouldn't have listened to my sister. Now we don't have anywhere to stay. She brought me all the way here from Savanalamar in Westmoreland to find a job, but there are no jobs here. I want to go home," Paulette said.

"You want to go back to that stinking place? Well, you'll have to go alone. I'm not going back," Pauline-the-twin said.

"Okay ladies, you don't have to fight each other. You can stay at my place in Glenworth until you find a job or decide what you really want to do. There's plenty of work, but sometimes it takes a while to find a good job. You'll have to check the newspaper daily until you see something that you like, but it won't take long. There're plenty of jobs out there How old are you?"

"We're eighteen," they spoke in unison.

"Okay, you're of age. Come with me and tell me more about yourselves. I have a large family at home, but you can make yourselves comfortable until you find good jobs."

Essie took the twins home with her. It took time for them to adjust to the new environment, and while they never talked much to anyone else, they whispered often to each other.

The third bedroom in the house at Glenworth was reserved for Essie at all times. However, there were exceptions. Sometimes the younger children like Bunny or Gena's kids slept with her to balance the total spacing of everyone in the house. When Essie stayed overnight at work, Myrtle occupied the room until she got back.

"Where is Momma? Has she left yet?" Junior said as he crawled out of bed in his boxer shorts, upper body shirtless.

"She just left," Myrtle replied.

"Where is she?" He rushed to the front door of the house just in time to see her carefully making her way down the lopsided, rocky steps that led to the roadside. Essie made sure each step was well placed before she made the next, like walking a tightrope as if she'd fallen before.

"Momma, do you want me to walk with you to the bus stop?"

"No, Junior, Karl...," Essie struggled to remember Junior's name.

"Junior, Momma."

"Thank you. Don't you have to go to work soon?"

"I finished the job I was working on yesterday. I'm waiting now to get paid. I might stop by there later. I got a new job, but I don't start until tomorrow."

"I won't stand a chance of getting a free lift to the bus stop if you're with me, Junior," Essie shouted back.

"Bye, Momma, take care and walk carefully, good luck with getting a ride to the bus stop." Junior watched his mother walking with pride and confidence in her nice outfit. As she almost disappeared into the distant curve, he noticed a red car stop for his mother. After a short conversation, she was invited to get inside.

Junior was pleased with the day so far. Essie got her wish and found a ride to the bus stop. If she got lucky, she'd get a ride all the way to work.

"Leonard, Leonard, Momma said to make sure yuh eat breakfast before yuh go to school. Okay?" Myrtle sat on the front steps, still yelling at the top of her voice.

"Leonard? Leonard did yuh hear me? Did yuh hear what I said?" Myrtle screamed.

"Leonard, Myrtle is calling you," Junior said as he poked his head into the boys' room and saw him getting ready for school. "Are you getting ready?"

"Yes, and I'm running late."

"I heard momma calling you to get ready hours ago."

"Yes, but I couldn't use the bathroom because Karl was using it first. I had to wait for him," Leonard explained.

"You need to wake up earlier so you can be the first to use the bathroom."

"Momma has to be the first to use the bathroom, then me, and then Karl, then anyone else can use it after that," Leonard responded.

"Boy, you like to give back answers? Do you think you're mister wise guy?" Junior asked.

Leonard didn't answer the question, at least not out loud, but he thought, *Yes I'm Mr. Wise Guy especially when compared to you.* But he dared not say it out loud unless he wanted Junior's wrath to come crashing down upon him that morning. Leonard learned how to navigate around trouble in his family. He knew what to say and when to say it and to whom to speak. He had bigger and better plans than they could imagine, so he didn't get lost in the day-to-day trivial matters.

"Yes, Myrtle, Junior said you were calling for me," Leonard said.

"Yes. Momma said to make sure that yuh eat breakfast before yuh go to school. She also left yuh school fare on the dresser with Betty." Myrtle knew why her mother refused to leave money in her care. Essie feared she'd buy cigarettes or marijuana

"Okay, thank you, Myrtle."

"Don't thank me, thank your mother. She was the one who got up early this morning and cooked breakfast for everyone. Yours is in yuh favorite plate covered up on the side of the stove. I've already eaten mine. Karl's and Bunny's are on the table. The rest will have to share theirs when they're ready," Myrtle explained.

Leonard rushed to the kitchen and peeped at his plate to see if the meal was worth his time. It was his favorite meal--yummy tempting ackee and saltfish with cooked green bananas and dumplings; he grabbed his plate and made his way to the table. It was certainly worth his time. He was late for school anyway so now he'd be late with a full stomach.

"Thank the Lord for what I've received for Christ's sake. Amen," Leonard whispered a quick prayer and after grace, he said to himself, "Thank the Lord and thank the hand." This was a table grace Essie had taught all the kids to say before they ate their meals. There were two things that she was strict about. One was for everyone to say their grace before they started eating because that would make a way for the provision of their next meal. She taught them that they should never take a meal for granted.

The next thing was that none of her boys were allowed to stay in their beds past sunrise. She believed that staying in bed taught boys to grow up to be good-for-nothing adults. She would have none of that in her family, and went around each morning waking all of the boys.

Most of the time, Essie made breakfast, prepared everyone's lunches and dinners, made a chore list and distributed money to those who needed it. It was an incredible feat considering that Essie only earned twenty U.S. every two weeks and yet accomplished so much. It was like the Bible story where the Lord used five loaves of bread and two fish to feed a multitude of people.

"Betty, Myrtle said that you have my money," Leonard said as he knocked and entered the girls' room.

"Yes, Leonard, there it is on the dresser, eight dollars. Momma said that it is for the whole week, so don't go finishing it now before time or else you'll have to walk to school and eat your books for lunch, okay?" Betty said in warning. She looked at the time and shouted to herself, "Oh my God! It's eight-thirty already? I have to get to work. Leonard, you're late for school."

"Yes, I know, I know. I'm out now, bye."

"Bye! Did you say happy birthday to Bunny?" Betty asked Leonard.

"Happy birthday, Bunny, may you live to see many more," Leonard shouted at the top of his voice, not knowing where Bunny was as he rushed through the door heading for school. He hoped he said it loud enough that Bunny heard him.

"Which one of these plates of food is mine?" Karl said as he went into the kitchen.

"The larger one is yours, Karl. There are only two prepared on the table. The other is for Bunny," Myrtle shouted.

Myrtle did all of her communicating with little effort. She heard everything that went on in the house and responded as needed, as if she was directing traffic.. Sitting on the steps was her favorite activity since dropping out of school and having open-heart surgery. Sometimes, if she did move, she joined a friend.

"Karl, did yuh find it?" she shouted.

"Yes, Myrtle. You can stop shouting now."

"Yuh ungrateful thing, yuh (you are so ungrateful).

Karl hurried through his breakfast and rushed toward the door to his welding trade school.

"Myrtle, my little sister, why are you so miserable?" He said as he tried to calm her, sensing that she was not pleased with his last comments.

"Don't touch me. I'm not yuh little sister. I'm older than yuh, yuh country bumpkin."

She remembered how rude he was to Essie earlier and used the opportunity to ask him about it. "Karl, seriously, tell me, why yuh so rude to yuh mother? Don't yuh know Momma really loves yuh? We all love yuh. Why're yuh still holding grudges against her?"

"Myrtle, why didn't you go and live in the country then and take my place?"

"Because Mast Tim a nuh mi Puppa, (because Mast Tim is not my father) that's why."

"Cool your heels. You don't know how evil that woman is."

"Well, if yuh don't like it here, why don't yuh go back home to the country and leave us alone?" Myrtle said, irritated. She was fed up with his rude, sarcastic ways.

"Myrtle, watch your heart, remember to take it easy on your heart. You worry too much about everything, even the things that don't concern you. Bye, I love you anyway. I'll see you in the evening."

"Did yuh remember to tell yuh brother happy birthday?"

"I was the first to tell him this morning. I told him before he even got out of bed."

"I love yuh anyway, Mr. Longelarla, Mr. Light Post Man." Myrtle teased Karl, indicating he was too tall and skinny.

Karl left feeling better that the conversation ended on a lighter note. He didn't like seeing his sister angry; he loved her. As a matter of fact, everyone, although not always in agreement with her, loved her unconditionally. In their eyes, she could do no wrong, especially since getting sick.

"Happy birthday again, Bunny." Like Leonard, Betty yelled out aimlessly.

"Thank you, Betty," a faint voice yelled back at her from an unidentifiable corner of the house.

"Bye, Myrtle. I'm leaving. I have an early appointment today. I'll be back in time to cook dinner this evening." Betty adjusted her dress, twisting it to the left and then back to the right, and headed out the door to fetch a cab for work.

"Did yuh get your breakfast? Momma left our food in the pot this morning."

"Yes, Myrtle, I shared out a little for myself. Thank you, darling, for reminding me."

"Okay, yuh are welcome, fatty bum-bum," Myrtle said, choosing a not-too-subtle way to tell her sister she needed to lose weight.

"Yes, my dear, I know. I need to lose some weight."

"Don't pay me any attention because yuh look good, my sister."

Betty waved as she crossed the street, fetched a cab, and headed off to her beauty salon.

Myrtle thought about delivering the remaining messages that Essie gave her.

"Pauline, Paulette, and Pauline-the-twin, listen to me. Momma said to wash yuh clothes today. I'll wash the boys' clothes, okay?" Myrtle shouted, hoping to wake up the others.

"Did anybody hear what I said? Pauline and the twins, Momma said to make sure to wash yuh clothes. I'll wash the boys' clothes, okay?"

"Oh no, Myrtle. You can't do any washing yet. You just had surgery not too long ago. I'll wash my clothes and the boys' clothes; it's not a problem for me. I don't feel comfortable with you washing clothes right now," Pauline said as she walked out to the front porch.

"Miss Essie knows I don't have any problem washing the boys' clothes. I usually wash Junior's clothes, so I'll just do everything together."

"What's wrong with me? Nothing is wrong with me, and if I want to wash them, I will. I've washed them before. If I'm going to die then I would be dead already." Myrtle frowned in disagreement.

"Oh no Myrtle, don't bother yourself. Let me do it this time, okay my love? Don't worry your little heart. Let me do it." Pauline continued to plead with Myrtle.

"Okay, next time I'll do it," Myrtle said. —Are the twins awake yet?"

"Yes, they heard you."

"Please tell Gena's kids that I'll share their breakfast for dem when they're ready, okay?"

"They're still in their room. When they're ready to eat, I'll have them call you. Miss Essie

124

made a big breakfast today. She really cooked a lot of food," Pauline said.

"Maybe it was because today is Bunny's birthday. That's one of his favorite meals and Momma always cooks a little special meal on our birthdays,"

Other than the extra cooking by Essie, this was a typical morning in the life of the large family at Glenworth.

Chapter 21

The closest activity to a family trip that Essie organized was when she took them to the beach on Easter.

"Great! We're going to the beach," Bunny said as he jumped up and down, clapping his hands.

"I don't have a bathing suit," Myrtle said frowning.

"What happened to the one Gena sent you not so long ago?"

"It's too tight now and it's ripped on both sides."

"Let me see it, maybe Gena... no Betty can fix it on her sewing machine."

"Miss Essie, I don't have a bathing suit either," Pauline said.

"Arm... Pauline, yes... Pauline, you can wear shorts and a close-fitting T-shirt or whatever. Let's just go to the beach, even if you don't go into the water."

"Do we have to come also, Miss Essie?" asked the twins.

"Yes, I want everybody to come. Is that too much to ask? I want to enjoy this Easter Sunday with my family and you're part of my family now. I've already bought spice buns and cheeses for a picnic. On our way, we'll stop by the shop to get one or two crates of sodas to drink," Essie explained, making it clear that although they were not aware of the family beach day, she'd been planning it for some time.

"Yeah! We couldn't celebrate Easter Sunday without buns and cheese. We're going to have a good time," Leonard said, rejoicing over the good news.

"We should be going to church to celebrate Easter Sunday. I'm not going with you. I'm going to church instead," Karl said, rebellious against Essie's family beach day plans.

"Jun… hum… Karl, you don't want to join us at the beach? It's going to be fun. Everybody will be there except you," Essie said, her voice sounding with regret.

"I don't care. I'm going to church. Easter is a church day and that's what I feel like doing."

"Okay, you can stay here and go to church if that's what you want."

She gave into his request because she knew how much he resented her for making him live in the countryside with his dad. She tried hard to make him happy and comfortable, but Karl openly swore that he would never forgive her until the day he died. He took every opportunity to show his resentment.

What Karl didn't understand was that when he treated her with disrespect, it didn't matter because she didn't feel it. Nothing said made her feel worse than she already did. If only she'd known that he had the same strong anti-country gene as she did, she would not have sent him.

She felt his pain. She knew what it felt like to be a big-city-minded person trapped in a small, country town.

The family headed off to Doctor's Cave Beach. When they arrived at the beach, they staked out a spot under a large almond tree. They laid out their blankets and towels and placed their picnic items under the shade

They jumped, splashed, dove, and swam in the ocean until their weary souls filled with satisfaction. They spanned, rolled, and played on the beach and their bodies glowed with the blazing island heat. They had a picnic lunch and a happy afternoon. They basted in the tropical inferno and worshiped the mean island sun as they frolicked around each other.

Essie's family was filled with the testimonial resurrection spirit as they amused themselves on that Easter Sunday. Essie was right-- they were having a wonderful time and it brought the family closer together.

While everyone was having fun, Essie went for a walk along the shores of the crystal clear ocean. She watched the gentle tides curling and rolling in toward the shoreline. The warm ocean water reached for her feet, while the sand tickled her toes as she strolled along the tropical aquatic playland. The waves rocked and changed directions with the wind. Kids and adults alike fulfilled their aquatic hearts' desires as they swam in the soothing water.

Essie stared at the long stretch of pure white sand beach that lay ahead. Sun-thirsty bodies all laid out in long rows of white reclining chairs with umbrellas standing near. The beachgoers soaked up the healing rays of the island sun.

She observed that there were other more lively and agile sun worshipers. Some were at the tiki hut; others sat around small, round tables watching the sunset as it painted new colors across the skies and seas. They were enjoying their mouth-watering hors-doeuvres, spicy beef patties, jerk chicken, and deep fried chicken wings, while others settled for a snack and a soft drink. Doctor's Cave was a picnic and sunbather's paradise.

She looked out into the spectacular, panoramic view of the coastline, looking seemingly still. Sailboats and glass-bottom boats floated along the ocean, and fishermen searched for their evening meal. She looked behind her at the offshore reefs and warm, shallow waters, ideal for snorkeling and for the underwater enthusiasts.

Essie peacefully observed her surroundings and smiled at the sheer beauty and serenity of her environment, the uniqueness of the people, and the natural attributes of the tropical island of Jamaica.

"Momma, we should do this more often," Betty said when Essie returned.

"I can't tell you how long it's been since I've been to the beach. It really rejuvenated my body and mind."

"Yes, it's true. We should do this more often. I need to teach the boys how to swim," Junior said.

"I can swim," Bunny said.

"I can swim, too," Leonard said, indignant.

"Well, yes, you both can swim but Don, Andre, and Breath don't know the first thing about swimming. I need to take them to the beach every Sunday to teach them," Junior said.

"I can swim a little but not that well," said Don, Gena's oldest son.

"I almost drowned today trying to swim," Andre said.

"Me too, I almost drowned," Breath agreed, joining the conversation.

"No! That's not true guys. Don't say that because if your mom hears it she'll die," Essie said.

"They're both exaggerating. Nothing happened to them, Momma. I was with them all day, playing with a beach ball on the edge of the water," Junior said.

"All in all, it was a great day. It has been my dream to see the whole family come out to have fun at this beach. I use to come here often as a young girl. I love this beach so much, it makes my heart glad to spend this day with my family," Essie said summing up the festive day, happily reminiscing about her childhood.

Chapter 22

One peculiar thing that Essie enjoyed was a good funeral celebration. She strangely had fun at funeral celebrations, but she wept at weddings.

Once, when a young man was playing behind an ice truck, he ran out into the street at the wrong time and was hit by a passing car. In those days, a truck full of large square blocks of ice visited Glenworth once or twice a week. They sold ice to those people who had no refrigerator. This truck was a large, open-back truck. It was like a supersized pickup truck. The pickup body portion was made of wood. One or two workers usually worked in the back.

They would use a large scissor-like ice holders to pick up the large, individual blocks of ice. They would move them around and slide them to the back of the truck so that they would be easier to divide into smaller pieces.

They would divide the ice with an ice pick, which was a long, pointed screwdriver-like tool. People would have their ice boxes and buckets ready to receive their ice for a small fee. These ice trucks would make many stops to effect these humble transactions.

One day, after the truck had made a regular stop, a young boy, Mike, a friend of Leonard and about the same age, decided that he would hop onto the ice truck while it was moving from one house to another. Mike was doing a good job holding on to the moving truck until it stopped at the next neighbor's gate. He jumped off and ran to the other side of the road without checking for oncoming traffic.

Unfortunately, he did not make it to the other side because a taxicab with very poor timing was coming at full speed around the side of the ice truck.

Essie was sad and empathetic to her neighbors' unfortunate loss. She went over to their home to give her condolences to the family. She also went to find out how she could help with the wake, also called a nine-night.

A nine-night was a traditional Jamaican way of cheering up a grieving family that had just encountered the loss of a loved one. It was an Afro-European-Jamaican traditional ritual that varied in its forms and styles.

In all its variations, there were two basic elements that remained constant: the acknowledgment and the showing of respect to the spirit of the deceased and the cheering up of the grieving relatives.

Usually, it was funded by the family that had encountered the loss, but oftentimes, a relative, a good friend, or even a church would step in and donate extra funds for the occasion.

The whole community, although sad and disappointed by the loss of a loved one, would partake in the celebration. It would start out slowly on the first night and pick up momentum over a nine-calendar-night period of time. By the time it got to the ninth night, the occasion would be in full swing. Sometimes, it turned out to be a big dance party with lots of liquor, food, and loud music.

Only the most committed nine-night followers would show up on the first and second nights. They were the "rumheads" or alcoholics some would say. Usually, they brought their own liquor with them, if it was not supplied by the grieving family.

They would meet at the gate of the deceased's home or in the front yard and form a circle where they would sing familiar songs that were unique to that occasion.

A typical nine-night song would be one called "Come We Go Down." It was Afrocentric, and it went like this:

Come wi go down, gal and boys, fi go broke rock stone [Let's get down, girls and boys, to break rock stones]. Broke dem one by one, gal and boys. Broke dem two by two, gal and boys. We go broke rock stones. If you mash yuh [hit your] finger, don't cry, gal and boys. We go broke rock stones.

While singing, they would be bending down with two or more stones in their hands, knocking them together and passing them to the next person. Each time the stones would go completely around, they would increase the speed. Sometimes playing this game while being fully drunk could be a serious challenge.

For other songs, there was a leader who read the verses of the song while the other members of the group would follow by repeating word for word whatever the leader would say. This style of singing was often referred to as a *Sankey*.

"Amazing grace, how sweet the sound." The leader would clearly and loudly speak the words of the song. Then the group would sing that verse and only that verse. They would sing it the best way they could.

"Amaaazing graaace, how sweet the soound," the group would sing.

"That saved a wretch like me." The leader would continue to read the words.

"Thaat saaved a wretch like meeee," the group would sing and then patiently wait for the leader to read the next verse.

"I once was lost but now am found," the leader would say.

"I onnnce was looost but noow am found." The group would faithfully sing the verse as it was stated by the leader.

A story was told of a Sankey at a nine-night ritual celebration that was being held in the countryside of the island. A respected leader was doing an excellent job of leading the group into the verses of the song. It was a large group, and all were singing and having fun. It started raining lightly, and the leader decided that it might be time to quit and go inside to get shelter. So he told the group, "I think it's time to quit."

"I thinnnk iiiit's timmme tooo quit," the group sang his words the best way they knew how.

"We must go inside to get some shelter from the rain," the leader warned.

"Weee muuussst goo inside to geeet some shelter from thee rain," the group sang the verse and waited patiently for the leader to lead them into the next verse.

"I don't know about you crazy people, but I'm going inside," the leader said arrogantly.

"I dooonn't knooow about yoouu craaazzy people, but I aam going insiiiide," the group faithfully repeated.

"Enough is enough, I'm getting wet, and I don't find this blasted thing funny at all. I'm out of here. You can find yourself another leader." He was fed up and upset, so he took off while the group was still singing his last words of warning to them.

Anyway, back to Essie, she loved to have fun at these nine-nights. She would usually show her support by baking a cake for the grieving family. She loved to bake. She would bake a cake every chance she got. If someone had a cold or the flu, Essie would offer to bake a cake for him or her. Everyone could rely on her.

However, if you asked her to make cakes selling, she would not do it. She enjoyed doing it for free. She would take donations to buy the ingredients, but she did not want to profit from the hobby.

She usually attended the last night of the nine-night. That was as much time as she could invest. Moreover, the last night was usually the big night with the Jamaican white rum, oxtail, curry goat, rice and peas, and power water. All of the favorite ethnic Jamaican foods would be there, plus all types of music, but mainly modern reggae. Sometimes it was like a big block party. If that didn't cheer up the grieving family, nothing else would.

Chapter 23

There was a story once told of a new priest who had to be disciplined by his superior at his second Mass. The new priest was so nervous at his Mass, he could hardly speak. After Mass, he asked the monsignor how he had done. The monsignor replied, "When I am worried about getting on the pulpit, I put a glass of vodka next to the water glass. If I start to get nervous, I take a sip."

So the next Sunday, he took the monsignor's advice. At the beginning of the sermon, he got nervous and took a drink. He proceeded to talk up a storm. Upon returning to his office after Mass, he found the following note on his door:

Sip the vodka; don't gulp. There are ten commandments, not twelve. There are twelve disciples, not ten. Jesus was consecrated, not constipated. We do not refer to Jesus Christ as the late J.C." The new priest was disciplined for his lack of judgment and his reckless behavior.

When it was time for discipline, Essie did not spare the rod and spoil the child. On the contrary, she did not hesitate to use the belt. The only good thing about it was she was prudent and knew when to stop. She believed that where parents went wrong with physical punishment was that they sometimes didn't know how far to go or when to stop.

Essie made sure that she got in at least three good strikes at her children when she was flogging or administering discipline to them. However, she only did that after two or three verbal warnings had failed. She believed that you should talk to your kids first. Let them understand your concerns. Let them know the danger that they faced if they didn't comply with the rules.

Essie told the story of "the man and his pony" to her children.

Once upon a time, a man and his son set out from the country to town to sell their pony to take care of their immediate finances. They had to go through several villages before they got to the auction. When they entered the first village, they were both riding on the pony. The village people were concerned about the pony. They shouted, "Oh, wicked people you are! How could you put so much weight on the poor pony? You should both walk and let the pony walk freely."

The man and his son complied. They were walking while the pony was walking free of the load. As they entered another village, the people of that village became concerned about the old man walking. They shouted, "Poor old man! Why waste the precious use of the pony while the old man suffers? Let the man ride the pony, and the boy can walk."

The man and his son complied. The man rode the pony while his son walked behind. As they entered the next village, the people of that village became concerned about the little boy walking while the strong father rode the pony. They shouted, "You cruel old man! Let the little boy ride the pony. You are strong enough to walk."

The man and his son complied. The man let the son ride on the pony while he walked behind. By the time they had passed through the final village and gotten to the market, both the man and his son, due to the urging of the village people, were now carrying the pony.

Essie would always close with the moral of the story. Her kids had to know what they wanted in life. They couldn't always listen to what other people said to them, or they would make fools of themselves.

Essie had an astute and peculiar way of administering discipline at times. She would suggest that the child that she was about to discipline go outside and choose the switch or belt that she would use for spanking. She considered this to be a psychological challenge that cleverly forced the child to think really hard, even if it was just for a second, about the bad deed he or she had done and to play an active role in assessing the degree of discipline that fit the behavior that warranted it.

One day, Bunny was told by Essie to sweep and clean up the front and backyard before she got back from work in the evening. Bunny, twelve at the time, ignored her request and went to play soccer. He spent all day with his friends and did not get back until late in the evening. When Essie came home and noticed that Bunny had not done what she had told him to do, she got upset and threatened to give him a spanking. She called to him, "Bunny...Yes, you Bunny, where are you? I would like to see you in the room." Essie told him in a very stern voice.

"Yes, Momma. I forgot to do the yard. I will do it tomorrow," Bunny started explaining as he approached his mother. He felt guilty because he was aware, from the anger in her voice, that he was in trouble. He tried to beat Essie to the punch, hoping to change the impending situation that he faced. "I'll do it as soon as I'm up tomorrow, I swear."

"Boy, what did I tell you this morning before I left?" Essie asked her trembling son.

"You said that I should sweep the yard before you get back home, Momma," he nervously responded.

"Did you do as I told you?"

"No, Momma, but I was going to do it as soon as I woke up tomorrow."

"What did you do all day while I was gone?"

"Nothing, Momma—no, I meant, I went to play soccer with my friends. Forgive me, Momma. I won't do it again. I swear. I won't do it again," Bunny begged.

"When I tell you to do something, I expect that you do it first before you go out and play. I don't mind if you go out and play soccer. What I care about is for you to be a responsible person. You can't make it in life if you are not responsible. Everyone has duties around here, and today, your duty was to clean the yard. Do you think that was too much to ask?"

"No, Momma. It was not too much. It was fair. Momma, you are a fair person. That's why I love you, Momma. God knows, I really love you, Momma. Please forgive me. I'll do whatever you

139

say. If you tell me to jump and touch the moon, Momma, I'll do it."

"Okay, son, jump and touch the moon for Me."

"Ahh…what?" Bunny's jaw dropped to the floor. His poor little heart skipped a beat. Shock and astonishment left his mouth wide open.

"Just trying to prove a point, Son. Don't make promises you can't keep." Essie smiled seeing the confusion on Bunny's face.

"Son, I love you, and that is why I want you to grow up to be a fine young man someday and get a nice job and do whatever you are hired or told to do. I'm going to spank you only because I love and care for you. Go outside and get me a switch now so I can give you a good spanking."

"Okay, Momma, I'm going now. I'm going to get you the best switch that I can find." It was, to him, like going outside to look for the bullet that was going to be used in his execution. It was one of his hardest tasks yet.

It didn't take Bunny long to figure out that this task was greater than the initial task of cleaning up the yard. *Why didn't I just clean up the yard before I went to play soccer?* Bunny thought. *Things would have been so much better if I'd done that; I wouldn't be faced with this difficult task at hand.*

After a few minutes of pondering, Bunny thought of a great idea. *Maybe I could spend the whole time searching for the right switch until it's time for bed. By then, maybe Momma would forget about it, and as soon as I wake up in the morning, I will take care of it. By so doing, I wouldn't have to*

140

deal with this whole scenario at all. Half an hour later, he was still in the backyard searching for the right switch to take to his mother.

Essie did not mind the length of time that it took because she knew that was part of the punishment. It was a twofold disciplinary action. This was the psychological part of it, and the longer Bunny pondered it, the more likely the point had been made that he needed to be responsible. Essie knew that in order for her kids to take her seriously, she had to follow through. It didn't matter how long it might take.

After an hour, Essie noticed that Bunny still hadn't returned, so she went outside to get him. When Bunny saw her coming toward him, trembling with fear, he shouted, "Momma, I'm looking for the best piece of switch I can find. I'm searching for the right size. I'm not going to stop searching until I find the right one. You deserve to get the right one. Momma, I'm not going to give you anything less. So you can go back in and let me take care of this. Please, Momma, go back in. I promise that I'll take the best switch to you. Don't worry, Momma, I know that I deserve a spanking, and that is why I'm trying to find a good switch."

Essie looked around in the backyard and noticed that there were many good choices. She could have just as easily grabbed one and started spanking him, but she was curious to see how far Bunny had planned on dragging out this two-minute situation. She became interested in the game that Bunny had going with her.

"So you are making sure that you get me the right switch, huh? Okay, son. I'll be inside

141

waiting." Essie turned away quickly. She could not help grinning. The thought of how her little twelve-year-old son was trying to outsmart her made her smile. She rushed inside, lest Bunny notice the sign of laughter on her face. She could not help thinking how her son was so bold to try an Oscar-award-worthy acting performance with her.

She started thinking, *This boy is going to be something special when he grows up.* However, it was her job to make sure that he got there, so she had to follow through even as humorous as she found the situation to be. She intended to give him a spanking.

Bunny continued to wander around the backyard until it was obviously time to go inside. He could not believe that his mother had fallen for his deceptive plan. *Maybe she has changed her mind,* he thought to himself. *Maybe she has forgiven me, or maybe she just gave up because I have outwaited her, and it wasn't worth her time waiting around for me. Maybe she had better things to do. Maybe I was the last thing on her mind among a million other things that she had to do.*

He felt victorious, although the end of his act had not yet played out. He felt like an athlete doing a ten-lap race who was ahead by five laps. He knew he had to face the music at some point. *What am I going to do now?* he thought. *Should I, after all this long wait, still take a switch to Mother? Then it would not be a victory anymore. No, I can't afford to do that. I've invested too much time and effort in avoiding being spanked.*

He began to realize that he had received more punishment in doing his extensive search for a switch than if he had just faced the music.

Bunny decided that he would let the chips fall where they may. He went inside and tiptoed into bed before anyone noticed him. Before long, he was fast asleep.

Not long after, Essie went to check on him with a strap but saw him sleeping. She looked at him with his adorable smile, but she could not let the other kids feel that this was a smart way of getting around what she demanded of them. She had to set an example for the other kids. Although she thought that it was cute how he had spent all that time trying to outsmart her and trying to avoid being spanked, she had to follow through.

She tapped him on the shoulder. When she knew he was awake, she raised her hands in the air and said, "Boy, I will give you a chance this time, but you must know that you are not smarter than me. Next time, you must do what I say. Okay, boy?"

"Okay, Momma. I'll do whatever you say," Bunny was relieved to know that the saga was over. It was funny, but he did not feel victorious. Instead, he felt bad. He knew that it wasn't worth it at all. He went back to bed and had a good night's rest. The next morning, he was the first to wake up, as he rushed to clean up the yard.

Essie was committed to administering proper discipline to her kids because she believed that if she didn't do the light punishment, then society or the cops would do the heavy punishment later in life. By then, her kids would unredeemable and out of control. She believed that parents were the ones who made a difference in society, and it was her job to teach her kids how to be good citizens.

***

Leonard, on his days off from school, used to spend most of his time across the street with his neighbors, the Mulgrave family. That was okay with Essie because the Mulgraves were a nice SDA Christian family. She knew that he could learn what it was like to live a true Christian life. They had prayer services twice a day and they would include Leonard. Essie would not question Leonard's whereabouts. She would automatically assume that he was with the Mulgrave family if he was not at home.

Leonard enjoyed spending time with the neighbors for the same reasons his mother thought he did. However, in addition to that, the Mulgrave family usually included him in their family dinner plans. If he spent the day with them, he could expect to have breakfast, lunch, and dinner. It was like a home away from home.

One day, Leonard's friends encouraged him to follow them to the ocean to go fishing. It was an intriguing idea, but he knew that his mother wouldn't approve of him going so far away without her consent. He refused to risk asking her just for her to say no to him. He figured that if he went with his friends, his mother wouldn't have to know. Maybe she would simply assume that he was at the neighbors' house. After pondering his options, he decided that he would join his friends. He was fourteen years old at that time.

"Sure, let's go," Leonard agreed.

So they went.

Unfortunately, Essie was at the door waiting when Leonard got home. She had been searching for him since getting home from work.

"Where were you, Bunny…hmm…Leonard?" she asked.

"Momma, I was at the same place where I always stay," Leonard lied to his mother with a very straight face, not knowing that she had already checked with the Mulgrave family and realized that he was not there.

"Where is that place that you always stay…hmm…Jun…hmm…Bunny…?‖

"Leonard, Momma."

"Yes, hmm…Leonard. I meant Leonard."

"At the Mulgraves', Momma."

"Come in here, boy. Let me teach you a lesson not to lie to me ever again. I was going to let you slide today if you'd told me the truth. But now that you are lying to me, I am going to teach you a good lesson."

"Okay, Momma, I was going to tell you. I was really with Ben and his friends at the beach. We went fishing, but we didn't catch any fish. I was hoping to catch some fish to bring home to make dinner," Leonard said. But he was too late. Essie was ready to discipline him for both leaving without her consent and lying on top of it all.

"Boy, go get me a switch. I'll teach you not to be deceitful."

"Okay, Momma. I'll do that." Leonard, just like the rest of Essie's kids, had learned a lesson from Bunny that it made more sense to go straight for a reasonable switch and get it over and done. Leonard rushed to the backyard and picked a small but reasonable switch and brought it to his mother. She took it from him and told him to hold out his hands. She gave him three very hard strokes on the palms of his hands and warned him never to do that again.

After it was all over, Essie sat him down and told him a story.

Once upon a time, there was a mother who had two small children, a five-year-old girl and a six-year-old boy. They each had their own bicycle but the girl refused to ride her bicycle by herself. She liked it when her brother pushed her so she didn't have to pedal or do any work.

However, her brother would rather riding his own bicycle and be left alone. He did not enjoy pushing his sister around.

One day, their mother warned them to be careful go to the back of the house because she had an expensive glass vase there that she did not want broken. If anyone should break it, they would get in big trouble.

The kids made sure to only ride their bikes in the front yard. One day, the boy was bored and decided to ride into the backyard. The worst scenario happened and his sister was there to witness the accident. The boy broke his mother's vase. He was so nervous that he did not know what to do.

146

His sister cried out, "Aw! Aw! I'm going to tell Mommy that you broke her vase and you're going to get in big trouble."

"Oh no, don't tell Mommy. I'll do anything for you."

"Okay. You'll have to push me on my bike around the house until I tell you when to stop."

"Okay, I'll do that. But when Mommy asks about it, please don't tell her that it was me who broke her vase."

"Okay, then get started," his sister said. —Come and push me around the house now." The boy pushed his sister around and around the house on her bike until he was tired. He tried to stop but his sister said, "Well I'm going upstairs to tell Mommy what you did."

The boy was scared and reluctantly continued to push his sister. This went on for weeks. His sister would boss him around and order him to push her on her bicycle.

Sometimes, in the mornings, she would sit on her bicycle in front of the main door to the house proudly waiting for her brother to come down and push her virtually from morning until night. Whenever he got tired, she would threaten to tell their mother about the secret.

One day, the boy came downstairs and saw his sister in her usual position. She said, "Come get to work. Her brother stood at the door observing how rude his had become.

He was fed up and started to wonder when it would stop. He knew he could not go on like that forever. His sister was turning into a little monster.

"Come on, get cracking now or else I'm going to tell mother about the vase," she said. Her brother just stood there thinking. He had been a slave for his sister. "Come on I said. Get to it now. Push me on my bike before I go and tell Mommy that you lied to her. You broke her vase and you're going to get in trouble. So get cracking now."

However, her brother had enough of her bulling. A big smile came over his face. Suddenly, all the stress and anxiety fell from his face.

Like a windshield wiper cleaning the dirt off the glass, the boy's smile wiped away the anxiety from his face. He could see clearly again. He decided that it was time to solve the problem himself.

"Why don't you push yourself around? I'm not going to do that anymore. I'm not going to let you boss me around. I'm going to tell Mommy myself that I lied and I'm sorry."

"Okay! Go ahead! You're going to get in big trouble," she said as he ran upstairs to tell his mother;

"Mother, I broke your vase and I lied and I'm very, very sorry. It was an accident. I didn't mean to break it. Please forgive me, Mommy." His mother turned to him and said,

"Son, I was looking through the window that day when you broke the vase. I knew that it was an accident.

I didn't say anything to you about it because I wanted to see how long it would take for you to confess the truth. I saw how your sister bossed you around, but I wanted you to learn the most important lesson of all. When you tell a lie, you become a slave to it."

Essie closed her story with a few final warnings. She told Leonard never to become a slave to a lie. It is best to be honest and face the consequence.

She explained that whenever he told a lie, he was actually giving up control of himself to someone or something else.

She explained that he would lose control of himself because he would have to continue using another lie to cover the previous lie. He would end up having to do this chain of lies each time he was confronted.

The original lie would be used to push him into a different state of mind. If a person wanted to get him in trouble, all he had to do was to force or trick him into telling a lie and then hold him to it.

This could not happen if he tells the truth in the first place. A lie can be more unnecessary work and energy than one bargained for or than one could have ever imagined.

***

Essie was somewhat lenient with Karl. He was the only child who had never really been disciplined by his mother. She felt guilty for letting him grow up in the country with his father. At least, he always try to make Essie feel guilty about it. He would remind her about it every chance he got.

Other than his bad behavior to Essie, he was a surprisingly well-disciplined child. He never got in any major trouble, and he was focused on becoming a successful person when he grew up. He bragged about how he was going to be a millionaire. He read many mind-empowerment books. One of his favorite books was *The Road to Becoming a Millionaire*. He was a self-motivated person who never got in any major problems or fights except with his mother.

If he hadn't carried such a strong grudge or hatred for his mother, he would have been considered the perfect child. However, his grudge was so strong, it consumed his very being and overshadowed any good that he had inside of him.

Myrtle was a firecracker, or the "bad kid" in the family. However, everyone loved her dearly. Essie had a special love for her also, but she was not afraid to discipline her when necessary. Essie knew however, that when she did, she would have to be ready for a big fight.

Most of the time, Essie would allocate the power to Junior, as he was the oldest. She allowed him to deal with Myrtle and most of the other kids when necessary. Essie seldom had to administer discipline to her oldest kids, Gena, Betty, and Junior. She sometimes had to discipline Junior as young child to get him to go to school. He never liked going to school, but he was a well-behaved child.

Chapter 24

Essie's favorite cake was the delectable, mouthwatering Jamaican fruitcake. She would make all types of cakes as needed for particular occasions. However, she loved to make authentic, enticing, scrumptious Jamaican fruitcake.

She would start with the bits of dried fruits and the individual components days before the occasion. She soaked the fruit in rum for days, and then, when it was close to the event, she would bake the cake.

If the cake was for children, she would omit the rum but would add a sweet, finger-licking glaze of icing after the cake was baked. If it was for grown-ups, she would go all the way with dark Jamaican rum and raisins—the whole shebang.

Essie would bake her delightful birthday cakes for all of her kids' birthdays. That was one thing her kids could depend on for their birthdays. It would read: "Happy birthday, so-and-so! I wish you luck and prosperity, Mom." Most of the time, she could not buy a gift, but she would be able to make a cake.

Betty turned eighteen years old and woke up to a joyous chorus of the famous birthday song from her brothers and sisters.

"Happy birthday to you. Happy birthday to you. Happy birthday, dear Betty. Happy birthday to you!" They all sang to her while she lay in bed.

"Thank you, guys. Thank you so much."

"You're welcome," they all said together like a chorus.

"Where is Momma?" Betty noticed that her mother was missing from the gathering.

"Momma is still at work. She stayed over because she got held up while preparing a surprise for your birthday," Junior said, lying to cover for Essie while she was in the kitchen doing some finishing work on the cake.

"Hope you live to see many more wonderful birthdays," Bunny said with a gleaming smile.

"I wish you the same," Karl said.

"May you have a wonderful year," Leonard followed.

"I wish you lots of prosperity," Myrtle added.

"I wish you good luck," Andre and Don said to their aunt.

"I wish you good luck too," Breath said, following his brothers' wish to their aunt. While they were still giving their wishes, Essie burst into the room with a luscious, sweet-smelling fruitcake.

"Surprise! Here is your cake that I baked for you. Happy birthday to you, my daughter. Happy eighteenth birthday."

"Oh my God! My birthday cake; you guys lied to me. It is a wonderful cake. I love it, Momma. Thank you so much. A birthday is not a birthday without one of your special cakes!" Betty shouted. She sprang out of bed to blow out her candle.

"Make a wish," Essie said. Betty paused and closed her eyes. She blew out the candle. She was happy, although she had not been given any other special gift. She knew that Essie's cake, made especially for her, was the best gift that she could have gotten on her eighteenth birthday. Essie made Betty's special day a delightful one. She gave her the best of what she could afford, and she gave it with the deep, caring love that came directly from a mother's heart. What more could anyone ask for?

Essie also baked cakes for any major occasion or celebration at Leonard's church.

His church members would look forward to Essie's contributions.

"Hey, Leonard, are you coming to this year's church harvest celebration?" a church sister asked him.

"Sure, I'm looking forward to it."

"Does that mean you'll be bringing one of those titillating fruitcakes that your mother makes?"

"I don't know as yet. I'll have to ask her."

"Oh! Please do. Don't forget to ask her to make a cake for harvest. You know how much we love her cakes."

"Okay, I will remember to ask her about it."

"It wouldn't be a harvest without your mother's oh-so-appetizing fruitcake. Mmm…makes me hungry just thinking about it. Remember now, don't forget, or else I will have to go and ask her myself," the church sister threatened as she walked away. Leonard told his mother about the church harvest celebration that was scheduled for three weeks away, and Essie gladly baked two large fruitcakes for him to take.

Essie also baked for school and community occasions. Bunny's class was having a school party, and the students were told to bring any food they liked. However, Bunny's teacher specifically instructed him to bring one of his mother's fruitcakes.

"Bunny, don't forget to tell your mother to send a cake for the class party," she reminded him. It was no secret that the teacher was more interested in the cake for herself than for her class. At the previous party, she had taken two-thirds of it home with her.

In fact, the whole community knew about and loved Essie's famous fruitcakes. In order to get a big turnout at a community party, one just had to advertise that Essie's fruitcakes would be there. That party or occasion would be a guaranteed hit.

Chapter 25

Essie got baptized within two months from that night after she astonishingly found God.

The only reason she was not baptized sooner was because she wanted to do one more thing. She knew she needed to get married to the man she really loved, the man God kept putting in her life every time she needed him most, the man who had been in her life from when she was a teenager, the man who was waiting patiently for her. Essie decided to ask for Tim's (Leonard's and Karl's father) hand in marriage before getting baptized.

When Essie asked Tim to marry her, he did not say a word. He was as silent as the day Essie left him. "Timothy Brown, the true love of my life, will you marry me?" Essie knelt, with her hands clasped in a prayerful position in front of her face, as if she were pleading for his forgiveness for any wrongs in the past.

She looked up at Tim as she asked him this life-changing question. She knew in her heart that she had done him wrong.

Tim did not respond. He stood still for a moment and looked down at her. He was swallowed up into her wanting stare. He looked up to the heavens. He was on the verge of breaking down. "Thank you, Lord," he said, his body shaking like one only did when a grown man cried.

He walked up to her and held her hand, gracefully raising her up from her knees. He was thankful to God for answering his pleading prayers from many lonely nights. He hugged her like the father did his son in the story of the prodigal son.

"Essie, my pretty lady, we started it together. So it is only right that we end it together. That's what good friends do; we wait for each other to catch up in life. I'm happy you came back to the arms that were longing for you. Having you as my wife will make me a happy man. You make my life complete. I can go to my grave in peace and with dignity."

"Tim, you know I wouldn't have it any other way. I love you. I always loved you, and I'll love you until the day I die," Essie promised him.

After she married Tim, she was baptized and became a true Christian. Essie insisted that everyone call her by her new matrimonial name: Mrs. Essie Brown. She no longer had repeated thoughts of suicide. She knew God understood all things. She knew that God had forgiven her for all her sins and made her into a new person.

The more Mrs. Essie Brown understood the Bible and the ways of God, the happier she became. Eventually, Essie became such a strict Christian, she was almost fanatic.

She would pray to God twice per day. She sang songs from the hymnal, read her Bible, and prayed from thirty minutes to as much as two hours early every morning for the rest of her life. She also did the same thing in the evenings. Essie praised God so much that it seemed as if she was trying to make up for lost time in her earlier life. It seemed as if she was making up for the times in her life when she was not a Christian. She could not get enough of serving God. When Essie found God, it was irrefutably the happiest time in her life.

Her husband, Tim, devotedly remained in the country, and she remained in the big city, as it had been in old times. Tim would roll out the red carpet for his adorable, gracefully aged Christian wife every time she came to the country.

Mrs. Essie Brown would do the same for her humble, country farmer husband whenever he came home to her in the big city. Some people were made to be different. But that didn't mean they weren't meant to be together.

Chapter 26

Essie's life took a significant upswing after she found herself. The first significant change in her life was made with her own two hands. She had lived her life as a strong, single mother until she married. She officially and proudly was no longer a single parent.

This much-needed change came a little late in her life. It was seemingly as late as the ironies mentioned in the lyrics of a song called "Ironic" by the very thoughtful singer, Alanis Morissette: "It was like a death row pardon two minutes too late...It was like a free ride when you already paid...It was like a traffic jam when you're already late...It was like meeting the man of your dreams and then meeting his beautiful wife..."

In Mrs. Essie Brown's case, it was like a woman who got married after living her whole life as a single mother, or it was like a woman who finally got a good father or stepfather for her kids but her kids were already grown.

Anyway, the point is that this change in Essie's life was late because most of her kids were already grown by this time. Nevertheless, it was a significant, incontestable change for her. Although grown, for the first time, her kids could say that they had a stepdad. One can never be too old to have a stepdad.

She had someone who swore that he would be there, for better or for worse, to lean on for the rest of their lives. Whatever was left of them.

These were simple things, but they were huge in Essie's eyes. It was as if she had been brokenhearted ever since Stedman and her best friend betrayed her twenty-five years earlier. She had been carrying her broken heart in her hands like a cracked egg the entire time. She jumped from relationship to relationship, and heart crumbled a little more each time.

But the buck stopped here. She could feel each crack in her heart fuse back together to make one uncluttered, trusting, beautiful organ. She could exhale and breathe easily again. There was no more gloomy, colorless world. She could see and enjoy the wonderful array of colors in the rainbows and in the fresh dew roses. Essie, at age fifty-four, felt complete and was ready to live, trust in love, and dream big dreams once more.

The next significant change in Essie's life was made possible by her miracle child, Gena. Gena, few years after stowing away to the U.S. on a cruise ship from the Bahamas, providentially married a wonderful and humble, down-to-earth American citizen named Wesley Dobson. Soon after, she was able to obtain her permanent resident status, which propelled her into the legal, working, taxpaying society in the United States. This also allowed her to travel back and forth to Jamaica.

This newly gained status elevated Gena's opportunity to see, firsthand, any problems that her family had. She would then try to solve each one if possible. She would travel with lots of goods for the family and continued to send barrels of food and goods as well. Gena invested a lot of money in her mother's home so that her family could live more comfortably.

Gena also helped with domestic affairs. She encouraged and financed Karl's wedding to his wife, Marva. Gena helped pay for Leonard's private-school tuition fees, so Essie wouldn't have to worry about it anymore.

Gena did so much for her family around the time when Essie had anathematized her past and opened her heart to a wonderful new way of life, that it appeared as if God began blessing her indirectly through Gena. It was like an efficacious cycle. God blessed Gina abundantly. The more Gena was blessed, the more she would return the blessings to her family.

One of the most significant things Gena did that helped to change Essie's life was to fulfill her promise to her. Gena had made a promise that she would someday pave the way for the whole family to travel to the United States where everyone could get a better and brighter future. She was not able to make her promise happen all at once, but she chipped away at it. She did whatever it took to get each person from Jamaica to the United States, one at a time.

***

The first person Gena brought from Jamaica to live with her in the United States was her younger brother, Leonard. One day, while she was passing by a private SDA high school in New

York, it dawned on her that there was a special visa called a student visa that was designed specifically for someone like Leonard, who wanted to become a doctor.

She thought this would be the perfect means of getting him started on the right track. He would leave one private SDA high school in Jamaica to go into another private SDA high school in the United States.

She stopped by the school to find out what was required to get her brother admitted. She got all of the required documents from the immigration office and mailed everything to Leonard for him to fill out, sign, and then take to the U.S. Embassy in Jamaica to obtain a student visa. Leonard, who had no prior knowledge or anticipation of traveling to the United States, was excited.

Leonard reflected on a time in his past when he had made a poor attempt with a neighborhood friend to stow away on a cruise ship to the United States. He was fourteen and happily attending Harrison Memorial High School. He had good grades in school. For three years in a row, he was ranked seventh in his class of more than thirty students, and he was third or fourth among the boys in his class of more than twelve.

He was the spitting image of his father, Tim. He was a reserved, skinny, tall, handsome boy. He was neatly dressed at all times. He was the only student who carried a briefcase like a young Wall Street executive. When all of the other students were carrying knapsacks and regular school bags, he was carrying a briefcase like he was the teacher rather than the student. He knew that he stood out and was mocked in the crowd, but he was proud to be different in that way.

One time, he made an unusual book stand in his woodworking class. It had the appearance of a pulpit stand and the shape of the stone tablet of the Ten Commandments. It had a place to keep a book open (hands-free) while reading. He brought the hands-free book stand and nailed it to his student desk. It was the only desk in the classroom with any such thing on it. When anyone entered the classroom, they could spot Leonard's desk. He would even travel, at the end of the school year, with his special desk to his new classroom.

Leonard also reflected on one other item, which he had made for his mother in his woodworking class. It was a wooden frame with a heart carved out in the middle and an arrow running through it like the cupid sign. He was proud of his handiwork and he took it home and gave it to his mother. His mother cherished and loved it. She hung it in the family room. The next day, when he came home from school, he noticed that it had been chopped into pieces with a knife or machete by his younger brother, Bunny.

Leonard was upset, but he understood the nature of sibling jealousy. Therefore, he forgave his brother for being only human. Leonard knew that there were many great fantastic untapped ideas in his mind that no one could destroy so easily.

This brings us to the time when his neighborhood friend, Joseph, decided to stow away on a cruise ship. Being a close friend, Leonard listened to Joseph's big plans and dreams, and he tried to support the idea as much as he could.

Eventually, his support went too far, because he was deeply involved in Joseph's plan.

He was not only a supporter, but a possible partner with him. The plan was that they would stow away on a ship to the United States and then find a relative, who would come and get them at the U.S. port. Leonard was comfortable living his life as a high school student with a bright future. He believed in a good education. His favorite quote was from Bob Marley: He said, "Emancipate yourself from mental slavery, none but ourselves can free our minds." However, if it was a safe possibility that he could be transported to the United States, he knew he would go for it.

When the time came, Joseph and Leonard excitedly packed their knapsacks with the basic things that they naively judged they would need to survive on their adventure.

They confidently headed down one night to the Montego Bay Seaport where a U.S. cruise ship was docked. However, once they got there, the reality of the danger that was involved became foremost in Leonard's mind, so he denounced the formidable but premature plan and canceled his intention and support.

Joseph was angry because he was intent on following through with his plan. Leonard left on his own and headed back home. Joseph reluctantly followed him. They decided that there had to be a better way to get to the United States.

When Leonard received the immigration package from his sister for obtaining his student visa, he was delighted and realized that this was the "better way" that he had been wishing for all along.

It was easy to see why he was very excited. The whole family was excited to see that another member of the family was about to set foot on U.S. soil, where impossible dreams came true. The family realized, for the first time, that Leonard might make it to become a doctor after all. Everyone cheered him on.

However, there was a negative response at his first try at the U.S. Embassy. After Essie and Leonard got up early that morning and went on a four-hour drive to the U.S. Embassy, they were in despair at having been turned down. The embassy gave no explanations or reasons. They simply stamped his passport book with a denial stamp and returned it to them.

Disenchanted and sad, Leonard sank into a despairing and melancholy mood. He felt like it was the day of reckoning, and he had fallen short of making it through the heaven's gate because his papers were stamped for condemnation to perdition. It seemed like the dream had died that day.

Oh no, Leonard's dream would not die so easily. His determination was too strong for the door to be miraculously opened and then suddenly shut on him like that. It would not happen without a fight.

Leonard encouraged his mother to take him back to the embassy the following week. During that week, Leonard also encouraged his mother to get an additional referral from his school, although it was not needed. Essie did obtained the referral and they returned the following week. They presented their documents to the embassy but were rejected once again.

Leonard, though dejected, pleaded with his heavyhearted mother to take him back to the embassy the following week. That week, they obtained a referral letter from the Honorable Howard Cook, the minister of education in Montego Bay.

They returned to the U.S. embassy, but they were rejected again. He did not give up. He believed that if he gave up, he would be giving up on his dreams and letting down Gena, who had faithfully done her part. He pleaded with Essie to take him one last time.

Although his mother was exhausted and tired, she attempted the trying journey one more time. This time, they had obtained a letter of referral from a local politician. Unfortunately, it did not make a difference. They were turned down again.

Leonard refused to let go; he was like a dog holding onto a bone. He begged his poor, and exhausted mother to try one more time. Essie reluctantly and cheerlessly gave in to her desperate son's plea. She didn't know how much longer she could go on with this failing venture.

However, she mustered up enough energy to go again. They gathered another referral from a different politician and headed to the U.S. Embassy one last time. She prayed and then said, "Lord, if it's thy will, let it be done. Amen."

Essie decided that this time, everything was totally in the Lord's hands and whatever the outcome, it was what the Lord wanted for her son at that time. They went inside the embassy and waited their turn. When they were called to the window, they presented all of the required documents. But sadly, the immigration officer opened the passport, saw the previous rejection stamps, quickly added another rejection stamp, and returned the rejected and seemingly condemned documents to them.

They were very sad because they knew that they had done all that they could do, and this must be the will of God at that particular time.

Essie was convinced that if the Lord had wanted her son to travel to the United States, it would have happened on the first attempt. She even blamed herself for questioning the will of God.

Leonard was also a strong Christian, and he believed that it was the will of God for him to travel to the United States and get started on his journey to becoming a doctor in order to do mighty things for the sick and needy. Why would God not want another pair of healing hands on earth? Leonard believed that it was God who had given him the unyielding drive and the starving appetite to become a physician.

He also believed that his mother was right. It was not the will of God for him to get a U.S. student visa at that particular time. "That particular time" was the key phrase that separated Leonard's belief from his mother's. Leonard believed the last time that they had gone to the embassy, it was not the will of God. But the following week, it would be the will of God.

Leonard convinced himself that where they had gone wrong was attempting to get a student visa a month too soon.

The will of God was for them to go to the embassy three weeks before the SDA school in New York reopened for the spring semester.

He tried convincing his mother of his logic, but she did not buy it. She was burned out over the situation, but she did, however, ask Junior to accompany him one more time to Kingston, where the U.S. Embassy was located.

That week, they did the old routine. They got a new reference from another reputable official and headed to the embassy; but it was like an excruciating curse was upon them, and they were appalled to be turned down once more.

Leonard could not believe what was happening to him. He knew this had to be the big break that he needed to move in the direction of his dreams. He believed that God wanted him to be a doctor to help save lives and be an important contributor to this world.

For the first time, his eyes were opened, and it really dawned on him that his dreams were delusional and were not going to be realized in Jamaica. It was at a time when only the richest and the best of the best were admitted to study medicine at the University of the West Indies. He was not in that category at all. He did not consider himself a top scholar, but he believed that, with hard work, he could do anything.

His motto in life could be seen in one of his favorite poems that said, "Heights by great men reached and kept were not attained by sudden flight, but they while their companions slept, were toiling upward through the night." Only sons of doctors, professors, and popular politicians got accepted, because, in Jamaica, the spaces for medical students were few and highly competitive. Leonard knew that he had no chance of fulfilling his dreams on the island of Jamaica.

Leonard did not accept that defeat. He asked his big brother to take him back the following week, but Junior refused to waste his time traveling four hours to and from the embassy to be turned down again. Leonard pleaded with for someone to take him to the embassy again, but they all refused. They encouraged their disenchanted brother to face the fact that it was not going to happen.

That week, Leonard went to his school library and did some research. He found out that dentistry was one profession that could not be done in Jamaica at that time. There was no dental program available on the whole island of Jamaica.

Leonard decided that this was what he would have to do to circumvent the system. He decided to tell the immigration officer that he wanted to do dentistry instead. Leonard was ready to go to the embassy the next week, but no one wanted to go with him. No one wanted to waste their time.

Leonard decided to go by himself. After having gone six times, he was not afraid. He understood the route and the procedure. He got up early that morning at around 3:00 AM to walk to the main bus stop to get the bus that would take him to Kingston.

Although he was the only one on the dark, desolate street, he was not afraid. He remembered what his mother had told him when he was ten years old.

She said, "Son, all great men will pass away sooner or later, and the new great man is still a child at your age even as we speak. At some point in time, society will look to your younger generation to fill major spots and roles. It's to your advantage to choose your roles now and choose wisely. They will need prisoners to fill jails just as they will need doctors to fill hospitals and care for the wounded, lawyers to fight for the weak and the innocent, and presidents or prime ministers to lead the country and the world. Son, the earlier you choose a future role, the better will be your chances."

After praying to God to help him choose, he believed that God wanted him to live to be a productive man and he would not die until the job was done. He felt that he had been chosen by God to be of service to mankind in the future. Therefore he had no reason to be afraid. The only fear Leonard had was that the immigration officer would not deal with him because he was a minor.

When he arrived at the embassy, he repeated all of the steps that his mother had taken. When it was his turn to step up to the window to speak with the disgruntled immigration officer, Leonard was ready to put it all out there on the line. This was his final attempt, and if he was going down, he was going down swinging.

He stepped forward and handed the interviewer his documents and said in an angry but polite tone, "Sir, I don't know what is the problem. I have all of the required documents and more. I intend to study dentistry in the future, and this profession is not available in any schools in

Jamaica. The high school that accepted me in the U.S. is waiting on me. Classes are about to start, and I'm still here in Jamaica."

As Leonard spoke, he was astonished to notice that the interviewer was not listening to him anymore. The interviewer went over to the other side of the counter to shuffle some papers, and he signed and stamped some documents.

Leonard knew that no one had ever done that before in all his previous attempts. In previous trips, the interviewer simply took his documents, read them, and then stamped a rejection notice right there without moving to the other side of the counter. Leonard was dumbfounded. Although he liked what he saw, he was afraid that the immigration officer would still reject his documents.

Although it seemed as if he was talking to himself, Leonard continued talking as if this was his judgment day and he was at the pearly gates talking for his dear life. "I don't know what is the problem. The school is calling me to find out what's going on. They are expecting me to join the class early. I have books to buy and school-related preparations to make…"

He was interrupted when the immigration officer stepped back to the window and told him to go through the side door. He was stunned. The immigration officer did not return the documents to him as they usually did, so that was another good sign. Also, he had never been told to go through that particular door before.

Leonard was thrilled but bewildered. He could not believe what was happening. He was about to get his esteemed student visa after all. He was amused to be getting his student visa at a time when everyone had absolutely given up on him.

The story was once told of a man who was traveling up a snowy mountain and stopped to rest for a minute. It was night and it was dark. Suddenly, he fell and started tumbling over the side of the mountain. Luckily, the hiker grabbed a branch as he was rapidly falling.

He hung on to the branch for dear life. He prayed to God to save him, and God answered and told the man to let go. The man was shocked and disappointed to hear that his beloved God, the one that he had always trusted, wanted him to let go and die.

The hiker was not ready to die, so he held on even tighter. The next day, there was a crowd of people standing on the road below. They were amazed at the strange sight of a man who was frozen to death clutching a tree branch.

Everyone was puzzled because they wondered why the poor man did not just let go of the branch. The road was only three feet below him. The moral of the story is that you have to trust and believe, but more than anything, you have to do your part so God can do His. Leonard surely did his part and more.

That day, he received the long-awaited student visa. Within two weeks, he migrated to the United States to live with Gena. He was now on his way to pursuing his medical career.

Essie was happy because she knew that she had a son who was a determined fighter just like herself. It reminded her of the incident that night when he was two years old and was running frantically out of the street so as to not get hurt by the taxi. She knew then that Leonard was a special person. She believed that Leonard was blessed by God.

***

After trying a few strategies to get her family members to the United States some successful, some not, Gena was finally able to file for her mother. It took longer than she liked. However, Essie's papers came through five years after Gena became a citizen of the United States.

By this time, Tim had died from renal complications. Therefore, Essie traveled to the United States alone. She became a U.S. citizen, which allowed her to file for the rest of her children, whom were all approved.

Gena was able to say that she had fulfilled her promise to her mother. The miracle baby was able to make a way for herself and then paved the way, against all odds, for the rest of her family. Gena was indisputably the unsung hero of Essie's family. She single-handedly effected a major upswing in the graph of Essie's life.

Chapter 27

Essie enjoyed a good nine-night, but she wept at weddings. Like everyone else who is happy to see their little baby grow up to adulthood and get married, Essie cried tears of joy.

Bunny was often called her "wash belly." This term indicates that he was the last child for Essie. He was now of age and was doing well for himself. Bunny lived with Joyce, who had been his committed girlfriend for over twelve years. They started a leather business together, which was growing rapidly.

Their leather business was turning a profit like Rumpelstiltskin turned straw into gold. They also had two young boys, Fern and Neil. They had long since moved out of Essie's house and had built a grand, splendid home of their own. They had everything that a young striving couple should have, except the blissful matrimonial title of man and wife.

"Bunny, when was the last time you called your sister?" Joyce asked.

"Who? Gena?" Bunny asked

"Yes, Gena. Who else would I be talking about? I don't care about anybody else. Don't get me wrong. I love all of your family, but I only care if you call your big sister, Gena."

"Does that mean that you care for Betty too?"

"I don't dislike her. It's just that we don't see eye to eye. I don't have a problem with anyone in your family. It is you who have problems with them. After all, Betty is your sister, not mine. I'm staying out of it, my dear love."

"So does that mean that I was the only one that she kicked out of Momma's house?"

"Bunny, as I said, I'm staying out of it. I only wanted to know if you called Gena in New York recently. That was all I asked. Why yuh chose to give me a hard time, I don't know. It's a simple question, with a simple answer: yes or no," Joyce said as she began to get irritated at Bunny's round-the-woods evasion of her question.

"No, if recently means yesterday, and yes, if recently means in the past six months. You see, my dear love, it depends," Bunny continued to dance around Joyce's question.

"I told yuh that yuh should go into politics. That's where you belong. I swear." Joyce was now convinced that Bunny was hiding something and that was the reason he was avoiding giving her a straightforward answer. She knew him too well. "Why yuh don't want to call Gena? She is always so good to you."

"I got tired of her saying the same old thing every time I call," Bunny confessed.

"And what is that?" Joyce asked, as if she didn't already know the answer.

"You know, the same old thing."

"So what's wrong with that? I don't see anything wrong with that," Joyce said adamantly.

"Wrong with what? I didn't say what the same old thing was, so now I don't know what you're talking about."

"Don't play Mr. Wise Guy with me, Bunny. Let's just lay it all out on the table. What's wrong with us getting married?" Joyce was tired of the mind games, so she spoke clearly about what was on her mind.

"Haaw! See, that's why you're so concerned about me calling Gena. You know that every time I call, she asks when we are getting married. She always says that it is time to make it official. She always says that it's never too late to get married. She always insists that we do it soon. She always says that she will help us with the wedding and so on and so on. I'm tired of hearing that. Our life is perfect the way it is; we don't need a ring or any certificate to seal our love for each other."

"Speak for yourself. My life is not perfect. I do, and I repeat, I do. As a matter of fact, I'll repeat it again, I do need a ring and a certificate to seal this love." Joyce was firm on the topic of marriage for the first since being together.

"You sound very fired up. When was the last time you called Gena? Now I'm concerned."

He stopped what he was doing in his workshop, located at the back of his home. He put his tools away and looked up into Joyce's face. Her guilty grin was from ear to ear. "Oh! That's what this whole thing is about? Gena is on my case again? I see. When did she call?"

"Yesterday," Joyce confessed with a big sigh of relief. A load of stress fell from her shoulders, which could be seen from the release of tension on her face now that it was out there in the open. "She said that she will help us with the wedding expenses if we need her help. She also has a lovely wedding gift for us already."

"We don't need her help with any wedding expenses. We'll be happy to accept her wedding gift—"Bunny was interrupted.

"What are you saying?" Joyce asked, holding her breath and with both hands over her mouth. She felt light-headed, as if she was about to faint. She barely felt her feet on the ground. Her two feet were not enough to keep her standing in an upright position. She felt like she needed at least two more. She was barely holding up against the cruel force of gravity.

"Hey, I got away for twelve years already, and our kids are now seven and eight years old. You guys have backed me into a corner, and I have nowhere left to run. Moreover, we have to get married in order to get the gift that Gena has already bought for us. Between you and my sister, I have nowhere to run," Bunny confessed to Joyce. Joyce ran and jumped into his arms with a joyous scream.

"So that's a yes?" she asked. Without waiting for an answer, she started screaming for joy.

"Wait a minute! Let's not go too far before I do this. If I'm going to do this, I have to do it right." He cleared away all of the stray pieces of junk that were on the floor. Then he quickly climbed up onto his worktable and swept the vertical column that lined the inside of the roof. With his hands stretched high, he retrieved a small black box. He had secretly bought it a few weeks back after speaking to Gena. He had left it there waiting for the right time to propose to his loyal lover and the loving mother of his two handsome boys, whom he loved so much.

He knew that he would know when it was the right time to propose to her. Today, the time was perfect. He swiftly but carefully climbed down. He clumsily went down on one knee and called out to his sons and workers to stop what they were doing so they could hear what he had to say. "Joyce, my love, I'm so sorry that I have been such a pigheaded, stubborn person. I should've done this twelve years ago when I met you. Thank you for staying with me and loving me, regardless of me, during all these years. Joyce, will you marry me?" Joyce was overcome with emotion and tears. She could hardly speak.

"Yes, my love. Yes, my love. Thank you. You stubborn fool. You know that I deserve this and I have been very patient. We both know it was time to do this. Thank you." Joyce was in tears of joy as she embraced her fiancé and dreamed of a brighter and stronger future together.

Joyce was active member in the Glenworth SDA church. Therefore, making arrangements for a wedding was not difficult for her. She had organized countless weddings before; she just had never had the opportunity to organize her own. She jumped right into the preparation for a medium-size wedding. The following day, Joyce was on the phone calling her friends and family to let them know the good news. She and Bunny were going to marry on May twenty-first of that same year.

"Hello, Christine, will you be my maid of honor?" Joyce asked as she called her best friend in Canada, whom she hadn't seen in over five years.

"Noooo! Say what? Noooo! I can't believe it. Wait a minute. I have to take a seat for this one. Are you kidding me, Joyce?"

"Would I kid you? Well, I kid you not. Bunny asked me to marry him finally!"

"Finally! Oh my God! I don't believe it. I gave up on him years ago. I thought that he would never do such a thing." Christine was bubbling with excitement.

"Well, you know what they say, 'What nuh dead, nuh call doppy.'" ("If he's not dead, don't call him a ghost"—meaning, never give up on a person as long as he or she is alive.)

"You can say that again, child. Congratulations! I would not miss it for the world. Let me have the date, dear Joyce, so I can make a request for my vacation at work. I will be there for sure."

"So that's a yes? You will be my maid of honor?"

"Well, let me put it this way. If you didn't make me your maid of honor, there was certainly going to be a big fight at your wedding, because I would personally come to Jamaica to rip off the dress of anybody else who thinks they have known you longer. How long have we been friends? From when our eyes were at our knees? Child, just pencil me—no, make that pen—just pen me into your lineup as your maid of honor."

178

"Thank you, Christine. I knew that I could depend on you. I will send you an official wedding invitation in the mail."

"You better do that, girl, if you know what's best for you."

"I will also fill you in on all of the major happenings as time progresses."

"Congratulations to you again, my friend. You deserve the honor. It's about time Bunny realized what a good woman he has by his side. Keep me posted, okay, Joyce?"

"I will, mon. I will. As soon as we put everything together, I'll let you know more. All right, girlfriend?"

"Already, you've made my day. Bye." Christine said.

Joyce hung up the phone, turned.

"Who will be your best man, Bunny?"

"Well, we know it won't be Mickey. We broke up our business partnership after he stole my client, and you know the whole story after that. It just wouldn't seem right to have him as my best man. He used to be a good friend, so maybe he could MC the whole program. You know how he loves to talk. He would be a great host."

"So who is left?"

"Well, weddings are about the showcase, so it's a matter of who makes the best showmanship, as far as I'm concerned."

"You're right, Bunny. I am with you on that one. That's a great idea. We need to call him early so he can get enough time to make f the necessary preparations."

"So you understand where I'm going with this?"

"Yes, man, I understand. I was thinking about him also as the best option."

"I'll give him a call now while we are contemplating it." Bunny picked up the phone and called his brother, Dr. Brown, in Florida. "Hello, Doc. How's it going?"

"Good so far. I can't complain. Who is going to listen anyway? I'm just here giving thanks for life and good health. How about you, Bunny?"

"I'm doing good, doc. As you said, just giving thanks for life and good health. How is the family?"

"My wife is doing great. However, all we are doing is working the shirt and blouse off our backs, and we still can't get our heads above the level we need to reach. I told you about the invention that I got a patent pending for recently. I sent it out to lots of companies, but it's not looking too good. None of them accepted my idea for a disposable dental floss holder. I was sure that it was the next big explosion on the market, but none of the companies are taking the bait."

"Well, brother, you just have to keep knocking on the door. One day, it will open for you. Just keep trying, my brother."

"Thank you, bro. So what's the latest? What's going on, my brother?"

"Well, I have some bad news...Haa! That hurts."

"What's that? Are you okay, bro?" Leonard asked Bunny.

"No, it is Joyce here slapping me silly in my head because I said that I've bad news."

"What's the bad news, bro?"

"I'm getting married."

"Wow! Wow! Woooow! I'm sooo sorry to hear that, bro. How did you let that happen?"

"Long story, my brother, but your sister had a lot to do with it."

"Who, Gena? No, not Gena again. I feel for you, my bro. I believe Gena is receiving some kind of commission for getting us all married. Obviously, she enjoys playing Cupid. I remember introducing Dolcina to her, and before you know it, we were married. I'm sure she had something to do with it also. We've been married now for four years, and I must tell you, bro, it's not as bad as it sounds. But I really expected you to talk your way out of tragic things like these. What happened?" Leonard joked.

"I did. I've been talking my way out of it for twelve years. Time caught up with me, my brother. I'm tired of running. I happily turned myself in for the penalty, whatever it may be."

"Well, there is nothing we can do about that now other than to warn your two boys not to take their girlfriends around Gena when they grow up, because the same thing could happen to them. What can I do to help in this dilemma?" Leonard asked after recognizing there was more to be said about the wedding.

"Brother, I would love for you to be my best man. If you don't mind."

"Hey, I'll be there, but only if you're going to have bulla cake and pear and irratid water [soda].

Just kidding, my bro. I wouldn't miss it for the world. My little brother's getting married after umpteen years. Even if I didn't do it for you, I would have to do it for Joyce's sake. I would be honored to be your best man. I'm going to start working on my speech. By the way, when is the wedding?"

"May twenty-first of this year."

"Let me jot it down so I can know what days to ask for at work. Don't worry yourself, bro, my wife and I will be there. You know that we'll use any excuse for a vacation anyway."

"Thank you, my brother."

"It's my pleasure. I'm very happy for my little brother stepping up to the plate. It's about time."

"It is long overdue, if I say so myself."

"Congratulations, my brother, may you have a wonderful married life."

"Thank you, my brother. I'll talk with you soon."

"Bye for now, bro." Leonard closed the long-distance call.

Bunny decided to also call Gena while he was at it and tell her the good news.

"Hello, who is this?" Gena answered the phone.

"It's your brother, Bunny. How are you doing today, my sister?"

"Hey, Bunny! Do you have good news for me? Believe it or not, I just had a dream last night about you. I dreamed that you were crazy happy, and you called me to tell me that you were getting married to Joyce. I was so happy, but funny to know that, I was the one in the white wedding dress, a pretty, fitting white dress. It looked so beautiful. Oh! The wedding was wonderful. Bunny, you know that I don't dream all the time, but when I do, that means something is up. You know that."

"My sister, did you have that dream before or after Joyce called you yesterday and told you that we were getting married?"

"No! No, my brother, Joyce did not call me yesterday. I did not speak to Joyce yesterday. I swear. I dreamed it. I dreamed it. Ha ha ha." She laughed. "Oh my God! I can't believe it. Congratulations, congratulations, my brother. Oh my God! My little brother is finally getting married. I don't know why it took you so long but better now than never. Oh my Lord! That is good news. So when is the wedding?"

"It will be in May of this year."

"Good, get it over and done. I'll be there. I have my outfit that I'll wear down to Jamaica, but I have to go and shop for something for the wedding. I have to call Joyce to see how the planning is going. I want you guys to have a wonderful wedding. I know that it's going to be good, just leave it up to Joyce and me, we'll put on a nice wedding. I have to buy Momma a nice dress to wear. I know Leonard will pay her fare to go to Jamaica. Maybe he could pay Myrtle's fare also. I'll speak with him as soon as I get off the phone. Did you tell him about it yet?"

"Yes, I asked him to be my best man, and he said yes."

"Good choice, we have to be proud of our doctor brother. Let people know that we have a doctor in our family. Don't be afraid to list him in your program as a doctor because we have something we can show off about. Our family is coming from afar, and we have to be proud of each other."

"Yes, I'm very proud of him, my sister. I don't travel to the United States much, but I did attend his graduation, so I know his credentials are real and authentic. Why would I not use it? I'm very proud of him."

"I'm proud of you too, my little brother. You are doing well with your business, and you have a nice, big house to enjoy with your family. You have a lot of reasons to be proud. I'm very proud of you. Congratulations, I'll be dancing at your wedding in May."

"Thank you. I must make some more calls to let everybody know about the date, because it is kind of short notice, but it is the best time for us to do it."

"Don't worry yourself. Do what's best for you. I'll let you go so you can call everyone. Don't forget to call Junior in Los Angeles to see if he can get time off from his job. Okay, bye, my dear brother. Love you." Gena ended the call.

She was happy to know that her constant urging of the young couple finally paid off and they'd be getting married soon. It pleased her heart to see couples take that vow.

Bunny decided to call Junior to see if he would be able to attend his wedding.

"Hello, Junior. This is Bunny. How are you and the family?"

"Hey! My brother, what's going on? I was talking about 'the I' (this is a Jamaican Rasta dialect that means –you/him/them- or it could mean me or my) the other day, man. I was telling 'I man's'(my) friend that I have a brother still living in Jamaica and he is doing much better than everyone that I know in LA here. Ya man. It is a true thing. He couldn't believe 'the I man' (my)story. Jah knows (God knows)."

"Really, which brother is that? Do I know him?" Bunny jokingly asked.

"You man. Is you 'I man' (I'm) talking about."

"Okay, thank you for those kind words, although they are not altogether true, but I have your back on that one. If anybody calls me to double-check on your facts, I will cover for you."

"Man, Bunny, you don't know how good you're doing when compared to other friends that I have here in LA who're suffering."

"Well, that may be true. I must thank the Lord, as my brother Leonard says, for keeping my head above the waters. I thank the Lord for being alive and well."

"Yes, man."

"Junior, your brother is getting married in May. Will you be able to come?"

"Which brother is that? You and I are the only lucky ones that're not married, that 'I man'(I) knows about. So who is getting married?" Junior but jokingly asked.

"Well, if it's not you, then it must be me."

"Oh my God! I'm so sorry to hear that. Don't tell me. Gena caused it? I knew one day they would gang up on you. You should have called me earlier, maybe 'I man' (I) could have helped 'the I' (you). You know what they say about marriage, right? It's a three-ring circus; engagement ring, wedding ring, and suffering. No, my brother, I'm just kidding. You did the right thing. To be honest, I found a nice lady here in LA, and as soon as I can, I'm going to make her my wife. Things are still kind of tough, so I can't do it just yet. But soon, I might be doing a little private thing myself."

"Oh great! I now believe that when you find the right woman in your life, you should give her the honor and respect that is due to her."

"When did you find that out? Yesterday?"

"You got me there, brother. But it's never too late to do the right thing, as Gena says."

"True thing. Congratulations, my brother. I wish you lots of luck and prosperity. I wish that I could attend, but this job is a new job and 'I man' (I'm) not taking any chances with it."

"That was what I wanted to find out. I'm calling everyone early so they can request time off from their jobs. I know that it will be difficult to make it happen."

"No, man. I've to be honest with you. I'm very happy for you, but I won't be able to make it. I'm so sorry, my brother."

"No problem, Junior. As I said, I understand. I have to run. I'm still making calls to everyone to let them know. So, bye for now. Love you, my brother."

"One love, my brother. Jah bless. Seen? You done know. Ya, man. (good-bye, may God bless you, you know I love you)" Junior spoke like

186

a Rastafarian, but he had never had a dreadlocks, although he had always considered himself as one in his heart. He said he was a true Rasta man in his heart, but he didn't have to wear natty hair or long dreadlocks to prove it. Only Jah (God) knew his heart. After they hung up, Bunny called Karl in Florida.

"Hello, Karl, this is Bunny. How're you and the family?"

"Hello, young man. How're you? Thank you for asking. My family is doing good the last time I spoke to them. Remember, they're still right there in Jamaica. I'm the only one that is here. I see them every six months or so. And you, young man? How're you doing?"

"I'm fine, my brother. I just called to see if you would be able to attend my wedding in May."

"Let's see, today is January 12. That means, you gave everyone less than five months to get themselves rearranged by dropping everything in a hurry to attend your wedding? Who came up with that date? I'm sure it was not you because I know that you know better than that."

"Maybe I got you at a bad time, my brother, but I just wanted to know if you were able to come to the wedding."

"I'm sorry, my brother, nothing personal, but I'm stuck here in Florida. Has nothing to do with work or the short time that you gave for the wedding. I have some things I have to take care of before I do anything else. It's just one of those things. However, I wish you lots of luck with your wedding celebration. Have a good time. Okay, brother. Sorry I can't make it."

"Okay, brother, I understand. Life throws us curveballs every now and then. Say hello to the wife and kids for me. Bye."

Bunny realized that calling each of his family members was not easy. He thought of calling Lela in Washington, but the last call with Karl drained him of his energy. He assumed that Lela was also most likely tied up and wouldn't be able to attend. She hadn't returned to Jamaica since she left ten years earlier. What made him think that a poor man's wedding was going to make her revisit?

The story was once told of a groom who took his wedding vows seriously. At the wedding rehearsal, he approached the clergyman with an unusual offer.

"Look, I'll give you one hundred U.S. dollars to change the wedding vows. When you get to me and the part where I am to promise to 'love, honor and obey' and 'forsake all others, be faithful to her forever,' I'd appreciate it if you'd just leave that part out." He passed the clergyman the cash and walked away satisfied.

On the day of the wedding, the bride and groom reached the part of the ceremony where the vows were exchanged, and when it came time for the groom's vows, the clergyman looked the young man in the eyes and said, "Will you promise to prostrate yourself before her, obey her every command and wish, serve her breakfast in bed every morning of your life, and swear eternally before God and your lovely, beautiful wife that you will not ever even as much as look at another woman, as long as you both shall live?"

The groom gulped, looked around, and said in a tiny voice, "Yes." The groom leaned toward the clergyman and hissed, "I thought we had a deal."

The clergyman put the money into his hand and whispered, "She made me a better offer."

On the day of Bunny's wedding, everyone was at the Montego Bay SDA church. Everything was going as scheduled.

Gena and her children, Myrtle, Leonard and his wife, a coworker of Leonard and his female friend from Florida, his mother, Essie, and other family members were all present.

Leonard was with his brother Bunny in the back of the church trying to keep him calm. He was overcompensating for his years of not seeing or spending time with his younger brother. He had a little white handkerchief that he used to nobly wipe Bunny's face every time he thought he was sweating.

He made sure that it was obvious that he was overplaying his role, and by so doing, he would properly measure up to the honored role of best man to his brother. He wanted to be the "best" best man that his little brother could have wished for. When they stepped out into the front of the church from the vestry, they could see the cheerful faces of Essie's family. More than anything, they could see the tears flowing down Essie's face. Essie was crying tears of joy at seeing her little wash belly giving his vows to his own family.

Essie always cried at weddings. Most mothers cry a little at their childrens' weddings, but Essie was unique in that once she started crying, she never really stopped until the ceremony was over.

Sometimes, even during the reception party, tracks of tears could still be seen on her face.

When the piano began to play the "Wedding March," she started sobbing. As the bride began walking down the aisle in her beautiful, flowing white wedding dress, one like Gena had dreamed about, Essie stood up to admire the bride even with her obvious tracks of tears. Gena tugged on her dress and told her that it was best if she took a seat because her teary eyes, along with the fact that she was the only one standing, were not appropriate at that time.

After a brief matrimonial ceremony, the minister said, "By the power vested in me, I now pronounce you man and wife. You may now kiss your bride."

Essie, still in tears, stood up and started clapping her hands. She caused half of the congregation to follow her lead, and they too stood up and started clapping in celebration of the newly married couple. Mrs. Essie Brown was very emotional at her kids' weddings, and she was not afraid to show it.

***

Essie displayed the same manner of affection and emotion at Leonard's and Dolcina's wedding, which was held at a church in the Bronx in New York City. This was two years after Leonard and Dolcina graduated from St. John's University. They were still living in New York at the time, so they elected to conduct their wedding at St. Luke's Episcopal Church of God in the White

Plains area of the Bronx. The church was filled with guests of the bride and groom.

Most of the guests that traveled a long distance to attend the wedding were of the bride's family. They came from London, England, as well as Kingston, Jamaica. Dolcina's mother, Mrs. Garwood, had lived in Battersea, London, for most of her life. She was comfortably retired and living in a nice flat in one of the newer developments in that area. The oldest of her two daughters, nicknamed Tat, but whose true name was Claudine Garwood, also lived Battersea, London, with her husband, Grant. Tat's daughter, Paulette, and grandson, Jonathan, lived with her. They all traveled to the United States for the first time to attend the wedding.

Dolcina's cousin, Novia McDonald-White, nicknamed Dawn, also attended the wedding. She was an Air Jamaica's air hostess and lived in Jamaica. She traveled to the wedding with her husband, Gerald, and daughter, Grace.

Leonard's family in attendance consisted of all those who were already living in New York at the time: Gena, Lela, Myrtle, Essie, and most of her grandchildren. Both the bride's and the groom's families sat together on the right side of the church in the front row.

Leonard and his best man, Andre White, were in a private room of the vestry of the church. Upon hearing their cue, they both entered the front of the church to stand beside the pulpit where they were expected to wait patiently for the bride to walk up to the front through the main central church aisle.

191

As soon as they reached the center of the podium, where they stopped and faced the audience, Essie stood up and started sobbing. "Oh, my son is getting married. May God bless and keep them…" But Myrtle grabbed onto her dress and gave it a gentle tug indicating that she should sit down and not draw so much attention to herself.

Essie sat down, but continued crying softly while whispering to herself, "may God bless him and his soon-to-be wife so they may have many, many children and grandchildren. Lord, you know that they can afford it. Lord, bless her womb, so they may give me many, many grandchildren, I pray, Lord."

Then the bridal song started to play, and Dolcina entered the church and walked down the aisle. Essie sprang to her feet again, this time to admire the bride in her lovely, flowing white matrimonial gown. Myrtle tugged on her mother's dress again, and Essie complied. After a somewhat long matrimonial ceremony, the minister said, "With the power vested in me, I now pronounce you man and wife. You may now kiss the bride."

This was the cue that Essie had been waiting for. She sprang to her feet and started clapping her hands vigorously. Of course, just about the entire church stood up and followed her lead. They all clapped and cheered. Myrtle tugged on her dress once again indicating to her that maybe it was time for her to take her seat, but Essie was in no mood to comply with Myrtle's or anybody's wishes.

She was not willing to entertain anymore restrictions at all. She was happy, although still in tears, and she was not going to contain herself any longer. With a joy like this, the world should know how she felt. Her emotions were flowing like a BP offshore oil leak gone bad that will not stop or cannot stop—at least, not by any simple means. Try as she may, Essie let all her emotions out that day, and no one could stop her—well, at least, not by any simple means.

She was letting the world know how she felt about her son, who had grown up to be a pharmacist and was now about to start his own family. Long after everyone else had sat down, Essie was still standing, clapping, and praising God for her son and new daughter-in-law.

Essie had a soft spot in her heart for weddings. Even when Karl elected to have a small, private wedding, after Gena insisted that he get married, Essie cried at his wedding also. There was only a handful of guests at the small church in Rose Hall. It was mostly family members and a few close friends present. It was just the way Karl wanted it.

However, when the minister said, "You may now kiss the bride," Essie burst out into tears of joy. Essie loved to see her children take that matrimonial vow. It meant that there would be more grandchildren on the way, and it pleased her heart to have lots of grandchildren. It could have also been something deeper that was psychologically explainable from other elements in her life.

Chapter 28

The day before Essie migrated to the United States, like an ordained African tribal chief holding a mysterious, ancestral clan meeting about the passing of the torch and secret traditional narratives of their forefathers, she called all of her children and grandchildren and set up a clan meeting.

They met at her home in Glenworth to discuss some issues that were important to her. She wanted everyone to be aware of the fact that, although Myrtle was already away in the United States, the house in Glenworth was hers.

She made it clear that she didn't have a will yet, but if she should die on that same day, the house and everything within it would be owned by Myrtle. She also made it clear that if she should die and leave a will behind, she would like for it to be read in the open over her dead body. She wanted to make sure there would be no confusion over her dying wishes or directives.

Essie also pledged that she would be enlarging the house in Glenworth. She planned to construct a second level on the top and make it look beautiful. She promised to do all those things as soon as she could while living in the United States.

Living in the United States was more exciting than she had ever dreamed. Essie gave thanks for her life in the concrete jungle, New York City, where the coldest day of the year averaged

32.1 degrees Fahrenheit (in January) and the hottest day was greater than 90 degrees Fahrenheit (any given summer day).

Essie was happy with her life. She believed that living in the United States justified her burdensome life of hard knocks and her formidable and tiresome hard work. She reflected that her daughter, Gena, was truly a miracle baby.

She was happy that she had heeded Reverend Paul Murray that day when she was sitting on the wall in downtown Montego Bay. Many decades later, Essie believed that the reverend had been sent by God to solve her sterility and other problems. Essie Brown thought that God sure had a funny sense of humor. She believed God was not always typical, but God was always right.

Like Karl, who inherited his anti-country feelings from his mother, Gena inherited her mother's gift for cooking. The only problem was that she only cooked once per year on Thanksgiving Day. Ever since Gena had made it to the United States, she never took the Thanksgiving holiday tradition for granted. When she thought of the Thanksgiving holiday, she, with admiration, thought about how far she had come.

Thanksgiving Day made her reflect on her past. She thought about the uncanny story that Essie had told her about her father, the Reverend Paul Murray. She thought about how her mother had struggled with her to survive. She thought about the many different homes she had to move from because she and her mother were forced out of some disgruntled man's home each time. She thought about the time when someone rudely threw

195

a container of urine in her mother's face because he wanted her to leave the home where they had been staying.

She thought about the time when a vicious tyrant of a girl, who lived in her apartment complex, terrorized Myrtle, Betty, and her every day when they passed through the gate to go to school. She thought about the endless mishaps in her life that made her believe that she would not live to see a brighter day. The list of things Gena had to give thanks for was endless, so she never dared take that holiday for granted.

Many of those challenging stories have already been mentioned, but the story of Essie having urine thrown on here needs to be told here. Gena was sixteen years old when her mother was considering giving up her apartment because of financial hardship. She had planned to move in with Mr. Livingston. She had not fully given up her apartment, but she had given her landlord notice indicating that she would be moving out within three months.

While Essie and Mr. Livingston were dating, Essie visited his home often. They had a good relationship, but it was a new relationship, so they spent most of their time getting to know each other. He knew that Essie had eight children, but he did not pay attention to that part of her life. He had not visited her apartment, but he had met a few of her kids before at different times and places.

Since Essie was living on a small salary and an even smaller savings account, which was rapidly dwindling, she started getting worried that eventually, she might not be able to pay her rent and take care of the kids' basic daily needs. Therefore, she went to Mr. Livingston to ask him a bold question.

"My dear love, life is getting so hard on me. I was wondering if I could stay here awhile until I get myself together."

"This is a big, three-bedroom house. I don't see why not, my love."

"I'll have to give up my apartment because I can't afford to pay the rent any longer. You won't have to give us anything other than shelter. I will be able to provide everything else that my family needs. I will be able to cook for you and the kids every day, so in a sense, it should save you time and money."

"I'm divorced and have no kids. This is a large house for just one person. I said it was fine as long as you keep the house clean and your kids don't tear my place down."

"Are you sure, my dear? I will have to give up my apartment, so I have to be sure that you don't mind sharing your home with me and my kids," she explained, making sure there was no misunderstanding between them before she went ahead with the plan.

"It will be fine."

"I never thought that I would have to do this, but sometimes life forces you to do what you have to do. I know that it will be a little inconvenient to you, but I'll make it up to you," Essie said with a big smile on her face.

He was not a man of many words. He was tall and handsome and had a light complexion. He also had curly black hair. His humble personality and good looks were what had attracted Essie to him. She had liked him a lot and was happy to know that she had found someone who was willing to take in both her and her large family. "Thank you, Mr. Livingston. You won't regret it," Essie said.

She started making plans right away to leave her apartment. She packed all of her clothes and the kids' belongings and started moving her furniture and miscellaneous items over to Mr. Livingston's home. Since she still had three months left in her apartment contract, she was able to move her things slowly, a little at a time. Within a month, she was able to move all of her stuff over to Mr. Livingston's house. However, the first time the family spent the night over at his house, he woke up the next morning like a man possessed with demons. To say he was in a bad mood would be a big understatement. It dawned on him overnight that a large family like this was just too much for him to handle. He cared for Essie but not enough to give up his tranquil lifestyle.

"What is the problem, Mr. Livingston? You don't seem too pleased this morning," Essie asked.

"Yes, you are right. I want my privacy back. This whole thing is just too much for me. I want you all to get out of my house," he said in a sudden rage.

"Oh, Mr. Livingston, you don't mean that, do you?" Essie asked in utter surprise and shock. She had ambitiously hoped that he was not another discreetly smooth-talking man in her life. Such men comforted her with empty, futile words.

However, when they were hit with the despicable reality of the first storm, they dropped her like a plate of hot potatoes coming from an overheated microwave oven and, like cowards, ran away, leaving her terrified and standing all alone holding the bag of useless promises.

"I don't mean that, really? See if I'm not dead serious." He ran for a container that was usually stored by the bedside to assist with urination overnight since the bathroom was outside of the house. It was used during the night when there was an immediate urge to urinate, and the person was not able to make it outside.

Mr. Livingston reached with one hand under his bed, grabbed the container by the handle, and threw the rancid contents at Essie's face. He went to the kids' room and tossed the rest of the urine at them. Most of it got on Gena's clothes, and the children frantically cried as he began yelling, "Get out of my house now, I say. I want you all out now." Mr. Livingston was raging mad They ran outside, hysterical, and watched as he angrily tossed their clothes and furniture out the door.

That was one of the worst days of Essie's life. She was humiliated in front of her kids. Luckily for her, she had not lost her previous apartment. She still had two months' time remaining on the lease, so she moved her belongings back into her old apartment that day. They were sad and disappointed to see that a man, who had gone to bed calm and collected, woke up like a raging maniac the next morning. It was like he had mysteriously turned into a werewolf overnight, and there wasn't even a full moon.

The experience shattered their egos, but it also made them stronger. It produced a stronger band of solidarity within Essie's family. They became determined that they would make it in life and change things drastically for their mother. No one ever spoke about that incident again, but it haunted Gena all her life. When she celebrated Thanksgiving, these were some of the things she gave thanks for overcoming.

Gena, anxious but exhilarated, started preparing for Thanksgiving about a week before. She was as about Thanksgiving as a little kid was anxious about Christmas morning and what Santa had in store for him. The only difference was that Gena was the Santa Claus of Thanksgiving.

She started buying the nonperishable items like seasonings. She also counted the number of people for whom she would be providing dinner. She called to see who in her immediate family had other plans and who was planning on sharing Thanksgiving with her.

After that, she called her friends and distant relatives to invite them to dinner. No one ever turned down an offer for Thanksgiving dinner by Gena, because they knew that she went all out.

"Hello, Jenifer, what plans do you have for Thanksgiving this year?" Gena asked her cousin and good friend.

"No plans, Gena. I've no plans at all. My kids will have to pretend that they are eating turkey this year because I have no money and no time to cook, my dear Gena," Jenifer said. She giggled a bit and continued, "But I know that you are going to be doing your thing, and I accept. You don't even need to ask. I have already invited myself."

"That is true, Jenifer. You're right. I am doing Thanksgiving this year, and I want you to bring the whole family."

"Thank you, Gena, but did you know that my mother is here with me too?"

"Shame on you, Jenifer. You have to bring your mother and, as I said, your whole family. I'm just getting ready to do my Thanksgiving grocery shopping, and that is why I'm calling you now. I just wanted to make sure that I know who is coming and who is not," she courteously explained.

"Count me in—no, count us in. We'll be there bright and early, or on time."

"Great! I'm happy to hear that."

"What should I bring?"

"Your appetite. Bring a big appetite, because you know me, I make a big dinner when I do this."

"I know. Lord, I can't wait, Gena. I'll see you at Thanksgiving."

"Please make sure that you do come, because I'm looking forward to having you in New York. It will be a lovely holiday get-together because I haven't seen you in a while."

"Yes, mon, no doubt, we'll be there."

"Okay, thank you. Bye for now."

They almost always joined Gena for Thanksgiving. Jenifer was related to Miriam in Mt. Salem. She was close in age to Gena, and they kept up with each other over the years

Gena knew that she was a great cook, just like her mother, so she was confident about the quality of food she prepared. She loved to impress her friends and family with her presentation. She retrieved the most expensive plates and glasses that she stored away all year. Thanksgiving Day was when she pulled out all of her best things, from dinnerware to clothes.

Gena was a flamboyant dresser. She was not afraid to wear bright colors and over-the-top hairstyles.

One peculiar thing that Gena did on Thanksgiving was to make sure that she invited a poor or needy person from the neighborhood to join the family for dinner. She would see someone standing on the street corner, on or around the week of Thanksgiving, and approach that person to ask if he or she had plans for Thanksgiving.

A particular young, black, American girl, who lived in the same building as Gena. She had a dirty, rugged look, like a person in need of some attention. Gena saw her sitting by the front steps of her building and approached her. "Hello, young lady. I'm Gena. We live in the same building. Did you know that?"

"Yes, I see you all the time."

"Yes, I see you too, and I noticed that you are not working, it seems. What plans do you have for Thanksgiving?"

"None."

"Oh! I'm having a large dinner on Thanksgiving Day, and I would love for you to join us."

"Where is your apartment? On the second floor, right?"

"Yes, I live on the second floor in apartment 2G."

"Oh! Okay, okay." She nodded her head as she acknowledged the information.

"My name is Gena, as I said earlier. What is your name?"

"My name is Teshana."

"So, Teshana, can I expect you to join us on Thanksgiving?"

"Maybe. I'm a little afraid."

"There is nothing to be afraid of because my family would love to have you join us for Thanksgiving. So please come by. I'm expecting you, okay?"

"Okay, I'll stop by," Teshana promised.

Like her mother, Gena could spot a person who was truly in need, and when she did, she was not afraid nor would she hesitate to approach that person. She would go do her business and bring a stranger home to rescue her from some kind of trouble.

One time she brought home a young lady and her a two-year-old baby, Sade. Ann Marie was walking downtown with tears in her eyes, so Gena stopped to find out what the problem was. She told her that her mother had been taken to a mental institution. As a result, she had been kicked out of their apartment by the landlord. She sobbed as she explained that she had no other family in New York and didn't know where the baby's father was.

"Where are your clothes and belongings?" Gena asked.

"They are at the apartment. The landlord changed the lock on the door, and I'm not able to retrieve them." She explained that she did not have so much as a diaper for the child, much less clothes for herself. Gena believed her story. It was easy to smell the strong odor coming from the baby, as if the child hadn't been changed for days.

"Okay, come with me to Conway. I can get you some basic stuff until you get your things from the apartment."

"Thank you. I have been trying to get in touch with the father, but he won't answer his phone."

Gena took the young mother and child to the store, located in downtown Manhattan, and bought them clothes and other basic necessities. She took them home to stay in her apartment and to sleep on the couch until they could rectify the landlord issue and find the baby's father, so he could aid in the support of his child.

It turned out that such a matter was not that easy to resolve, and therefore, Ann Marie and her baby spent a longer time living with Gena than expected. Even Ann Marie's mother was released from the hospital into Gena's care. Gena never minded helping whenever she could. She was a concerned citizen like her mother. She had a unique way of caring for other people's problems. There were few people like Gena and her mother in this world, who truly cared about people in need. Gena lived a simple life, so she could use the excess to help someone else who was worse off than she was. Gena was the Mother Theresa of her own little world.

On the night before Thanksgiving, Gena was all fired up. She went through her checklist to make sure she had enough of everything needed for the big day. It was like a one-woman machine had been turned on, and she was about to put it into gear. She started cooking the night before. She seasoned the meats and made all of the cold side items, such as the potato salad and fruit salad, and whatever little things could be made ahead of time. She never allowed her mother to lift as much as a finger.

The one-woman machine never needed help, not even from her mother. She believed that, in order for the dinner to have her special stamp on it, everything had to be made by her. She enjoyed the fact that she could do all of the kitchen work while her mother sat down and was waited on for a change.

Essie never complained because she was growing weary of the kitchen work, since she had done nothing but that all her life.

Gena made sure to turn in early to bed because she knew that she had to get an early start in the morning. She made sure, however, that all of the pre-Thanksgiving preparations were completed and everything was in place for the next day.

While everyone else was asleep at 3:00 AM on Thanksgiving morning, Gena was up bright, alert, and ready with excitement in her eyes. It was Thanksgiving Day, and she was about to work her magic. She fired up all of the kitchen aids and appliances: the stoves, the oven, the microwave, and the pressure cooker.

She started working like crazy on tiptoes, making sure not to wake anyone before the right time. She enjoyed being the ghost of early

Thanksgiving morning. She moved around swiftly but silently like the fairy godmother of Thanksgiving, working with her magic fingers in the dawn of her favorite day.

By the time everyone was up in the morning, Gena was well on her way to the dinner. Most of the items were already cooked, and what was not cooked was on schedule. Gena had everything on timers. That day, she was dedicated to the kitchen, moving from one thing to the other. She was like an orchestra conductor, directing the pots and appliances to produce great musical flavors. She moved flawlessly as she conducted the meal all day in the small kitchen.

By late afternoon, all of the various dishes were done and waiting for the dinner presentation. As friends and family began to arrive, they were greeted with the tantalizing aromas of delightful foods waiting to be consumed. Everyone made their way to the living room to socialize and catch up on the holiday happenings but with a hungry, watchful eye on the kitchen activity.

By 5:00 PM, the house was full of people. Gena rolled out her Thanksgiving presentation kit. She used her best dinnerware to serve her guests while explaining where each piece had been obtained, and the cost and stories behind it, which most guests had heard many times before. They lent a listening ear anyway, as if it was the first time, because they knew that was what came with the exquisite meal. Gena went all out to impress everyone with her personalized service.

The guest enjoyed her delectable Thanksgiving dinner, as they chatted up a storm.

Everyone—men, women, and children—was having fun. This was what a good Thanksgiving was made of: friends and family enjoying themselves, appreciating a good meal, and giving thanks for a good year of health and wealth. It pleased Gena to see everyone enjoying her handiwork.

It pleased her to see her family in particular. She enjoyed the sight of her family, who had struggled over the years in Jamaica, now getting the opportunity to indulge in one of America's finest holiday celebrations and enjoy a worry-free time and good food.

This was what she had dreamed of as a child when she fantasized about a better place and a better way of life for her and her family. She didn't notice that it was a lot of work. It was more fun than it was work.

Essie also enjoyed her daughter's handiwork. She knew how cooking a good meal made one feel inside, because she had been there and had done again many times in her life. After all, Gena had inherited her natural talent for cooking from her, and she knew that it was a great feeling to see how much others appreciated your cooking. Essie offered to help her with the cleaning up, but Gena refused her help.

"My daughter, the dinner was great. I especially enjoyed the turkey. You are a wonderful chef, just like me. I'm proud of you, my daughter. I'm proud of you in every way," Essie said to Gena after her first Thanksgiving dinner in the United States of America.

"Thank you, Mom. I'm glad you enjoyed it," Gena said.

"Can I help with the cleaning up? There are lots of dishes and things to take care of. I would like to help you now, if you don't mind."

"Yes, I do mind. I don't want you or anyone in the kitchen. I'll take care of all this myself. I've been cleaning as I go along. I have my system of doing things. Thanks for the offer, Mom, but I'll do it myself." Gena cleaned up the kitchen after she bid everyone good night one by one.

"Thank you, Gena. The food was excellent. I enjoyed everything, especially unique collard greens and stuffing. You must show me one day how your stuffing is made," Jenifer said. "Thanks again, but we have to go."

"You're welcome, my cousin. It was fun having you and your family for Thanksgiving. Thank you for coming. We'll talk on the phone. Drive carefully and be good."

"Bye, Gena. Thanks for having me," Teshana said.

"My pleasure. Did you enjoy the dinner?"

"Yes, I enjoyed everything. I especially loved your sweet-tasting pumpkin pie and your to-die-for baked macaroni and cheese. I also loved your succulent oxtail. I loved everything. Now I'm as stuffed as a turkey. Thank you for inviting me."

"You're welcome."

Essie was thankful for sharing her first Thanksgiving holiday in the United States with her daughter and the rest of the family. She had a lot to be thankful for. One thing was being able to live and experience her first Thanksgiving Day in New

York City. She was also thankful to have experienced her first Independence Day on July 4th in the pleasantly hot, humid Big Apple.

Chapter 29

As mentioned, Essie enjoyed her first Independence Day holiday in New York City. It was a sight to behold. She was starstruck by the amazing scene of the blazing, starry skies and the heavy vibration of the blasting of the hidden cannons.

It was unbelievable what was happening in front of her eyes: the wonderful, starlike formations of fireworks. She gazed in awe at the instant blossom of the flaming rosebuds in the sky. She gasped at the ignited rainbow rays spitting fire and cracking lights of all shapes and sizes into the sky. She was amazed at the geniuses at work and the inventiveness of mankind.

She was at the muggy humid Central Park display of fireworks with her Bible in hand. She had a serious case of culture shock. There were thousands of people gathered to watch the breathtaking display of fireworks. Essie had never been in any one place that had so many people together. More than the fireworks, she was amazed at the number of people who were gathered together in one common location. She was overwhelmed but happy to be a part of the celebration.

It dawned on her that she shared the same goals and aspirations as every one of those sightseers. She shared the same appreciation of American history. She was, after all, an American at heart, and in just a *few* years, she would be a true

American by naturalization. The thought of this destined gift brought tears of joy to her eyes.

The fireworks were made for her. Although there were thousands of people, she felt gratified that the fireworks display was being performed just for her. It was her welcome party. She had a brand-new life and a clean slate in the United States. The skies were the limit, as far as she was concerned. It was like it was her first birthday, and she was being reborn in the United States. This was her birthday party, and the others were there to share in her celebration.

The fireworks represented everything that Essie believed in: the right to freedom, the right to a better life, and most of all, the right to be all one could be. It represented the God-given right to be. That night, Essie saw more than fancy high-tech lights and fireworks. She saw what it meant to be an American. It was the right to be. To be left alone, to be loved, to be one's true self, to be free, to be treated fairly, to be respected, to be strong, to be proud, and most of all, to be all that one could be. When Essie looked around and saw the kids celebrating and having fun while the grown-ups celebrated a great country that stood up and fought for what it believed in, it brought tears to her eyes.

Essie was impressed with the lighting of the Christmas tree at the Rockefeller Center in Manhattan a few weeks before Christmas. She celebrated her first Christmas in New York by attending the Christmas tree lighting ceremony. This is a New York tradition that started in 1933. She stood in the midst of downtown Manhattan with her Bible in hand to witness the spectacular lighting. She was impressed with the large crowd that turned out to witness it, just like she had. Christmas had always been special for Essie, but now it meant even more. They say that when you are in love, everything looks brighter and better. Well, Essie was in love with life in New York City, and even Christmas seemed better than it had ever been. As the tree was lit and the various groups sang touching Christmas carols, tears came to Essie's eyes.

As if that was not enough, Essie attended the Dick Clark's New Year's Eve Celebration. Although it was very cold, Essie enjoyed the experience. She was amazed at the large crowds that these occasions drew in New York City. She did not stay long, but it was important to have experienced and been a part of a great ritual of the Big Apple.

Essie was happy and proud living in New York City. After all, she was in the city that hosted the most distinctive landmark that greeted millions of immigrants in the late nineteenth and twentieth centuries. The Statue of Liberty was every woman, like.

Essie took the time to admire her new homeland. She went for a walk with Myrtle in downtown Manhattan. They strolled through the illuminated hub of the Broadway Theatre District, the major center of the world's entertainment industry.

They stood at one of the world's busiest pedestrian intersections, as Essie admired the famous Times Square that had been referred to as the mother of all crossroads and the ultimate crossroad of the world. Essie smiled as she thought about the small, T-shaped crossroad back in Cascade where her life had started.

It made her think about the time when she stood at the crossroad in her tiny village of Cascade and wished to fly away to a larger and better world. She was thinking then of a big city, but never in a million years would she have thought that she would be standing in the midst of Times Square.

Essie observed the Manhattan skyline with its universally recognized skyscrapers and nodded her head repeatedly. "It is true," she said to herself as her eyes caught the Empire State Building, "New York City is truly the home to some of the tallest buildings in the world."

She saw a large, colorful, computer-generated sign on the side of a building. It read, "Be bullish when you're on Wall Street." Her mind drifted to a piece in the newspaper she had seen earlier that day about the New York Stock Exchange. She thought about the fact that God had spared her life and had given her the wonderful opportunity to roam through the busy city streets of Manhattan, the financial capital of the world.

She was not sure what it all meant, but she was sure that it had something to do with lots of money flowing in and out of the Big Apple.

Essie had no regrets. She had seen it all, and it was all worth it.

***

At first, Essie lived with Gena in one apartment in New York City. She enjoyed it, but that situation did not last for long. It got even better. Essie got her own apartment next door to Gena. When Gena did her regular supermarket shopping, just before she headed into her apartment, she knocked on her mother's door first to drop off groceries or to stop in to make sure that she was doing well. For Essie, having an apartment next door to her daughter was the most convenient situation a mother and daughter could've had.

This was made possible by Gena, of course. Gena was able to apply for an apartment for her mother because Essie was now a U.S. citizen. Essie was doing so well that she was able to start helping all of her kids and grandkids, who needed her help financially.

Essie was still a Christian fanatic, so to speak. She attended her SDA church, Ephesus SDA Church, located close to her. She learned the route to her church well. She attended every church service, both the weekend Sabbath service and the midweek Bible study. In addition, she conducted her regular, one-hour early morning and evening devotion services at home, with or without company.

One difference between her Jamaican and American devotions was that she sang her hymns louder and with more confidence, although she was now more painfully off-key than ever. Just like a self-proclaimed or self-ordained minister, she also read more verses from her Bible. Her prayers were longer, as she prayed for all of her kids and grandkids. She prayed for each person individually, and sometimes she included the president of the

United States and people involved in the latest current event of the day.

If one thought that Mrs. Essie Brown used to praise the Lord a little too much while living in Jamaica, they would be shocked to know that she, joyously and unapologetically, praised God even more while living in the United States. She really had a lot of reasons to pray. Before, she used to praise God because she thanked Him for forgiving all her sins. Now, Essie praised God for blessing her so abundantly.

Along with getting the opportunity to praise God and go to church regularly, she was able to take better care of her health, since she went to the medical clinic monthly.

Before this time, she did not take proper care of herself. She was too busy working and worrying about other people's concerns. Her philosophy used to be that she was old and could die at any given time, whereas her kids' and grandkids' concerns were primary to her at all times.

She still believed that her family's concerns were primary, but she realized that she was not that old and she wanted to live a long and healthy life. Essie realized that life was worth living and that she had a lot to live for in the remaining phase of her life.

Her health care became a serious part of her daily concerns. She kept up with all of her doctor's appointments. She never missed an appointment for anything in this world. She arrived at least one or two hours early for all of her doctor's appointments.

She was aggressive and compliant when it came to anything health related.

When she first arrived in New York, she looked like an old woman, although she was only in her late fifties. She looked frail and sickly and appeared as if she was on her way to her grave. She walked slowly, and she bent over using a walking cane.

In her sixties, she looked twenty years younger. She walked briskly and strongly, and she spoke and moved around with spunk and energy. She felt for the first time in her life that she was really living. At age sixty-five, she even considered getting her driver's license so she could purchase a car and drive herself to church. It was like Essie came alive in New York City.

***

Essie found a church buddy named Julia Gomez, who was born in Honduras but grew up in Puerto Rico. She moved to the United States when she was in her early twenties. She had been a member of the Ephesus SDA Church for over thirty years. They met one Sabbath after church services.

"I'm Julia Gomez, but everyone calls me Tia."

"I'm Essie Brown. You can call me Sister Brown."

"I noticed that we always walk to the train station together after church, but I juwsally take the number two to downtown, and I think that jer route is somewhere uptown because juw juwsally go to the uptown side."

"I do live in the uptown direction, but only one stop on the train from here," Essie replied with a smile.

"I see juw every Sabbath walking to the train. Haf juw ever noticed that we always go that way after church?"

"No."

"Really?"

"I usually don't pay any attention to the people around me when I'm walking. There are too many people on the streets. If I pay attention to them, I'll trip and fall, and I don't want that to happen to me again. It happened once before when I was crossing the driveway of a Catholic church uptown."

"I wouldn't like that to happen to juw either, sister," Tia said with genuine concern for Essie. "Anyway, let's wolk, tolk as we head to train stacion, jes?" Tia's strong Latin accent escaped her as she got more comfortable with Essie.

"Yes, okay. Let's walk," Essie said as the two Christian ladies started to walk toward the subway. Tia was short with a medium frame. She was not too fat, but she was definitely not skinny. She had a pretty Puerto Rican look with a light complexion and long black hair. She had a slight Spanish accent when she spoke, but she spoke clearly.

As they walked together, Essie seemed almost twice as tall as Tia because Essie loved to wear her high heels when she went to church. She was dressed in an off-white two-piece skirt and blouse suit, with a small black purse in her hand. Essie also had a simple but sophisticated white hat on with her hair tucked neatly inside it. They walked slowly as they got to know each other.

"Sister Brown, how long haf you been in New Jork City?" Tia asked.

"I've been here for about five or six years now. I don't even know anymore what the exact time is. My sister, this head of mine is not the same anymore. I can't remember anything."

"That's all right, Sister Brown. We're at that age where nothing is the same anymore. Sometimes I don't even remember my address and phone number. It takes me a while to collect myself before it comes to me. Nothing comes easy anymore."

"We're old birds. We have to get used to it. How long have you been in New York, Sister Tia?"

"I've been here for over thirty years. I used to live in the Bronx by East Tremont Avenue. That area was getting too bad for me, so I moved to upper Manhattan, an area they call Spanish Harlem."

"I heard about Spanish Harlem. How's it living there?"

"It's okay. It's better than East Tremont Avenue. I live in one of the newer buildings. It's clean and nice and semi-gated. Jew should join me for lunch one of these days," Tia said.

"Oh, I'd love that, Sister Tia," Essie said as she accepted the lunch offer.

"I live alone now that my three kids are grown and living in different places."

"What happened to your husband, Sister T.?"

"I don't haf one anymore, Sister. We've been divorced for over fifteen years. I caught him in bed with my best friend. I never talk to him ever again. I was so hurt that I never got around to dating again. I just serve God. He makes me happy. Sometimes I wish that I had a man in my life to help me when things got rough, but I've passed those days now and my kids are all grown. God's the man in my life now."

"My husband passed away years ago, but I live with my daughter, Myrtle. I share an apartment with her and her son, Dean. I also have six grandkids living with us. It's a lucky thing that we have a large apartment to accommodate everyone. I wouldn't have it any other way. I love living with my grandkids. They make me feel alive."

"How do you like living in this city, Sister Brown?"

"Oh, I love it. I'm a big-city gal by heart. I love the people. I love the food. I love the senior citizens' services everywhere. I love everything. I love my church. I don't like the long walk sometimes, but I love everything else. I like how everything is close by; for example, the supermarkets and shops are just across the street. God has blessed me with lovely kids and a good life."

"Praise the Lord, sister! Praise the Lord! I love it too, sister. I love everything. I can't complain. Sometimes the weather gets too cold, but I make sure I dress warm before I come outside."

"Me too."

"How are jer kids, Sister Brown?"

"God has blessed me with eight kids. They're doing very well. I have my beloved daughter, Gena, who I called my miracle baby. She was the one who filed for me so that the rest of my family and myself could leave Jamaica to live here. I'm so proud of her. She lives next door to me, and she has her own hair-dressing parlor, which is doing very well.

"I also have a son who is a doctor. He lives in Florida. I go and visit him sometimes. He pays my fare anytime I want to travel and he sends me money from time to time. All of my kids stay in touch with me. Thank God. I have a son in Los Angeles doing well and going to church, a daughter in Washington who has her own nursing home, and a son and a daughter in Jamaica. My son has a big house in Jamaica.

"Well, there is a long story about his house, but someday, we will sit down and talk about that. He also has his own leather craft business that is doing very well. My daughter in Jamaica also has her own beauty parlor business." Essie raised her two hands high in the air. "Thank you, God! You've blessed me and all my kids. Sister Tia, it wasn't easy as it was me alone, but thank God, He was by my side. He saw me through it all."

"Praise God, Sister Brown. God is good, and He is mighty. I know because I had to call upon Him many times to help me also. I was a single mother of three kids. I got a no help from their father who is a big-time journalist now living in England. But now they're doing very well."

"Where are you from, Sister Tia?"

"I was born in a place called Tegucigalpa in Honduras. My parents migrated to Puerto Rico because of a big business opportunity when I was five years old. I grew up in Puerto Rico until I finished schooling there. I worked in a major hotel as a manager for many years. I came to live in New Jork for a better income, so I can better take care of my kids. I did some home-care nursing assistance until I retired. Now that my kids are grown, I'm just taking it easy and serving my Lord."

"Sister, they say, 'Many rivers to cross,' but we found our way over. We are both women of substance. Don't ever forget that. What we have done, so that our kids could have a better life, no one could imagine."

"Jes! *Es verdad*, that is true, my sister. That is so true."

"Have you ever been back to Honduras?"

"Jes, I have gone back a few times. However, when I go, I don't usually stay long. I used to visit my grandparents there, but they haf both passed away, so I haven't been back since."

"Do you like Jamaican food, Sister Tia?"

"Jes! Sister Brown! I love jerk chicken, I like how they do oxtail, and I love the ackee and salt fish."

"I can make you a Jamaican special one of these days. Did you know that I was a personal chef for some very high-profile celebrities, including Roger Moore from the James Bond movie? He stayed at my private cottage resort twice in Jamaica, and he loved my cooking."

"Really? Jew must be a great cook, Sister Brown. I tell you what. We will trade dinner treats.

221

One day, you can cook jer Jamaican special for me, and then I'll cook you a Honduran Latino special that my grandmother taught me."

"Okay, we'll do that soon, Sister Tia," Essie concluded. By this time, they were standing at the mouth of the New York subway. They continued trading stories with each other. When they heard the heavy chuckling and loud rumbling of an approaching underground train, they realized that they had been in the same spot for a long time, so they decided to bid each other good-bye until next time.

"Okay, Sister Tia. Travel safely and take care of yourself until we meet next week."

"Okay, Sister Brown, here is my number. Jew can call me anytime if juw want to talk. I'll be here."

"Oh! Yes, that's a good idea. Take mine also," Essie said as she traded her telephone number with Julia. They remained friends and church buddies.

Chapter 30

In addition to enjoying the induction and matriculation into New York City, Essie enjoyed traveling to different areas in the United States and Jamaica. She traveled frequently, especially on special occasions, to Washington DC to see her other daughter, Lela. Lela was married with one more child by the name of Shana. She had her own nursing-home business. What is the real story about Lela? Did she do well without Essie playing a major motherly role in her life?

She grew up in a wonderful family with Essie's cousin, Miriam, who lived in Mt. Salem. Miriam was close to Essie. In fact, they were like sisters. They kept an open communication with each other over the years. Essie had promised herself that as soon as she could, she would request that Lela be returned to her or, if for any reason Miriam could no longer care for her daughter, she would not hesitate to take her back home into her family where she belonged. Essie always made mention or comments about her eight children, as if Lela was living with her.

She did that so she would keep her in the foremost of her mind. She also did that so her kids would realize that they had another sister, who might not be living with them but was in every way a part of them.

The undeniable, ever-satisfying fact was that Miriam provided, at almost all stages of Lela's growth, a much better life than Essie had to offer. Therefore, there was no need to worry about her well-being. She was in good hands. Lela had a great childhood with two siblings from Miriam, Donna and Mavis. They grew up closely, like biological siblings and best friends. Nevertheless, when Lela felt like reaching out to her larger family unit with Essie, she knew she would always be welcomed by everyone. She would drop by her biological mother's house to pay her a brief visit. She knew that she had the best of both worlds. However, more than that, she knew that she was fortunate to be living with the family that could care for her better.

Lela also had very good friends in her life. They lived in a more affluent neighborhood than Essie's family. Her friends were of a higher social class than would be expected if she had been living with Essie. She went to an affluent private high school, known as Harrison Memorial High School. It was the same SDA school that her brother Leonard attended.

Lela wanted to become a registered nurse. She pursued that goal until she met a wealthy businessman, a butcher, and who owned a large, lucrative butcher shop in the center of downtown Montego Bay. She was in love with him, and she got pregnant and bore her first of two girls with him. Luckily, she was still able to graduate from high school. However, she halted her nursing career plans to help run her kids' father's business.

Lela was not completely satisfied with her life. The relationship was rocky because of his constant infidelities and external affairs. He refused to commit solely to her in the form of marriage so that they could build a solid future together. She felt insecure and doubtful of the direction of her life. That was when she welcomed Gena's offer to travel to the United States to start a brighter future.

Once she got to the United States, she tried many different jobs, but nothing worked out well for her. She also tried a few short-term relationships, but none were substantial until she met Damian, a black American ex-army officer. They dated for a while and moved in with each other.

They later married and had a lovely baby girl named Shana. They started a home-based nursing home business that held up to eight patients. Funny how life is--Lela, who always wanted to be a nurse, was now working like one for her own business. They bought a house as soon as their business began turning over profits.

Her two oldest daughters, who were left behind in Jamaica, grew up to be successful young ladies as their father filed for them and they migrated to Pennsylvania to live with him. One became a registered nurse and the other became a hotel manager. Lela's youngest daughter also did well in high school. She was at the top of her class and began proving herself to be a true scholar. Lela's life was wonderful and successful. However, not everything was well. Lela was stuck in paradise.

At the time Essie became a U.S. citizen and filed for all of her kids, Lela was already married to, and had one child with, Damian. It was assumed that Damian would do the right thing and file for his wife to become an American resident. Therefore,

Essie did not, and could not, even if she wanted to, file for her.

Damian had a unique philosophy, however. He believed that he had been used and badly hurt by a former lover, and he vowed to himself that he would not let that happen to him again.

This time, he stayed in control of his relationship instead of letting it control him. He genuinely loved Lela, but he believed that if he supplied her with everything she needed, except a permanent United States resident status, then he would be in full control of his relationship.

If only Essie knew Demon's philosophy—so sorry, the name is Damian, just a slip of the pen—she would have advised Lela to allow her to play this one oh-so-very-vital motherly role in her life by filing for her along with the rest of her family. As it stood, it seemed like Lela was happily stuck in paradise.

***

Essie enjoyed traveling to Florida to visit her son, Leonard, who was married to Dolcina. Both were pharmacists. They lived in Florida practicing their profession.

Leonard always dreamed of having a significant impact on the world. Today, he braggingly considered himself as one of the most ingenious inventors the world had never met. About three years after he graduated from St. Johns University pharmacy school, he stumbled upon a simple but r unique idea at the time.

One morning after brushing his teeth, he lazily thought of skipping the next step, which was to floss his teeth. He struggled with the idea that it was such a cumbersome activity of forcing one or both hands into one's mouth with a floss string. As a pharmacist and a promoter of good, healthy living, he knew that it was a necessary means to a healthy, cavity-free mouth. He thought to himself, *Why is it so unpleasant to floss one's teeth?*

He knew if he found it unpleasant, then half the world or more should be experiencing the same problem. Shouldn't it be a more streamlined process? Shouldn't there be a convenient tool for flossing, like the toothbrush?

Why, in 1993, were people still using their bare hands in their mouths for the purpose of flossing? No wonder there were so many kids and adults who were refusing to floss on a daily basis.

Leonard thought about a motivational book that he had once read in New York. The book made mention of the old popular phrase, that says, "Build a better mousetrap, and the world will beat a path to your door." It dawned on him that he had stumbled upon one of the most overlooked frontiers: the improvement of the process of flossing teeth without using the caveman-style method of using bare hands and a flossing string.

He was excited about his idea. He knew that it would only be a matter of time before this oversight was realized by the rapidly growing healthcare product industries. He knew he had to jump at it fast. He sat down to create and map out a tool that he believed could make better use of the flossing string that was on the market. He mapped out a disposable dental floss holder and made a call to Inventors of Florida, a company that advertised its services on TV. He set up an appointment to see the consultant of new inventions, and then he called his wife, Dolcina.

"Duls, I have an invention idea. Check it out." Leonard showed his wife his drawing of a disposable dental floss holder. "What do you think?" he asked Dolcina with excitement in his voice.

"Lord, Leonard, get rich quick so we can travel the world."

"Yes, that will come afterwards, but I want to know what you think about my idea."

"Well, I'd use it, and therefore, I guess many other people would want to use it also."

"So are you saying that you like it?"

"Sure, why not? It's an excellent idea."

"Well, is it good enough to pay over three thousand dollars to get it started? I've already called the Inventors of Florida, and they explained to me about their fees and the general procedures. I have an appointment set with them. I'm serious about getting it done."

"Lord, more money spending again. I hope you can make some good money out of it," she said. Then she thought of a dim possibility. "What if someone has already done it and it is already on the market?"

"Good question. We can ask the consultant when we get there on Monday."

"What time is the appointment?"

"It's at 10:00 AM."

On Monday morning, both Leonard and Dolcina attended the appointed meeting with the Inventors of Florida. The consultant was excited. He thought it was an ingenious idea. Leonard asked about his wife's question, which he could not answer a few days earlier.

"What if someone has already thought about it and invented it and it is already on the market somewhere out there?"

"Oh, that is simple. It is our business to know before we start. Before we get started on anything, we first have to do a complete, thorough patent search. This patent search will confirm or deny if you are the inventor or not of this idea. We do an excellent job here.

When we say you're the inventor or not, we back it up with the proof," the consultant explained to the excited couple.

They made a down payment on the process and initiated all of the necessary paperwork. They waited a few weeks for the patent search to be completed. There was good news. There was no existing patent available on the market. Leonard was excited. He knew that it was the greatest oversight of its time. He was overjoyed because he felt victorious to be the one to discover this.

He knew that he was about to change the world into a better place, even if it was only in the small area of flossing. Imagine millions of boys and girls using his disposable dental floss device all over the world. He knew that he was born to be a great human being, and he had done it. He had discovered a better, more acceptable, and easier way to do dental flossing, and he was going to allow the experts to show him how to bring his idea to life.

Within a month, the Inventors of Florida got engineers to make an artistic and detailed official drawing of the prototype of the product. An application for patent-pending status was filed and obtained. It was suggested by the experts that a patent-pending status was the way to go instead of a patent. It was the expected thing to do if you needed the company to build and market your invention for you.

A neat introduction package that described the product was put together and marketed to twenty-five large companies. Included in this group were Johnson & Johnson, Proctor & Gamble, and Pfizer, along with a few other popular companies. At least fifteen of the twenty-five companies returned a response of no interest. The other ten held on to the idea and gave it serious attention for a few months. They kept up communication with him of the progress of their board meetings and follow-up decisions. They also kept him abreast of the method of assessment of his product as it might benefit their company.

There was one particularly interested company that took his idea all the way to the top level of their evaluation system before they came to a sudden denial decision. It was a disappointing, heartbreaking feeling for Leonard to know that none of the twenty-five companies chose to accept his idea. Most of the companies said that it was not worth their time and effort because they were involved in bigger and better things.

Leonard decided that his shot at greatness was not in the invention department, so he decided to sign up at Nova Southeastern University to do a postgraduate PharmD program, a doctor of pharmacy degree. He felt that he had a better chance of impacting the world with his enhanced medical skills and knowledge.

Exactly one year later, Leonard walked into a drugstore and was shocked to see the same product he had invented, with a little improvement of course, on the store shelf. How ironic was that? One year before, when he marketed his idea to some of the largest companies in the United States, no one thought it was worth their time. Yet, a product or concept that was not in existence was now a new item all over the country. Leonard burned with fury. Someone must have stolen his idea. They did not even think of giving him credit, not to mention a reward.

He took his case to a patent lawyer, who agreed that it was too much of a coincidence not to be considered. He advised that it would take time and money to fight his case. The lawyer suggested that he take each company that was now producing and marketing the product to small-claims court to fight his case for less cost and expense.

Leonard, for whatever reason, did not follow through on the fight to restore credit for his idea; but to this day, whenever he sees a dental floss holder, it still infuriates him. It hurts him to know that he was the bona-fide inventor of that idea, but he did not get his due credit. One thing he knows for sure is that his mother, Essie, was correct when she said that her son was going to grow up to be a great man someday.

Leonard did impact the world in a big way; the only problem was that the world hadn't recognized him for his great idea. He knew that it was only a matter of time before the world discovered his idea, but at least he had impacted the world by improving on one of the basic hygienic behaviors and habits.

Immediately after the completion of his doctor of pharmacy degree, Leonard published a few medical articles in a popular, internationally distributed pharmacy news magazine in an effort to reach a wide range of people with his newly acquired healthcare knowledge; but this activity did not heal his pain and disappointment. He wanted to make his mother proud, and he knew that his invention of the disposable dental floss device was the thing to do it. However, Essie was proud of her son and was happy every time she visited him and his wife in Florida.

***

Essie enjoyed visiting her oldest son, Junior, in Los Angeles. He was married to Patricia. Junior worked at a Kodak firm fixing Kodak machines and did well for himself. He also started attending church regularly. He had dropped the Rastafarian mentality believed in Christ.

Essie enjoyed traveling back and forth to Jamaica to visit her daughter, Betty. Betty had been living with her in New York, but decided that she

232

wanted to return to Jamaica to attend to her beauty parlor business.

When Essie was in Jamaica, she also visited Bunny, who was married to Joyce and now had three children: Fern, Neil, and a sweet little girl named Zena. They also had an adopted daughter named Brenda. Bunny refused to migrate with the family to the United States because his leather business was doing well in Jamaica. Bunny was content to be in Jamaica. He and his wife, but mostly his wife, traveled to the United States every now and then. He obtained his permanent resident card, as had his two sons, Neil and Fern, like the rest of Essie's family.

He also later became a local politician and a respectable notary of the public of Jamaica.

***

Essie also visited Karl, who was a popular manager in the food and beverage department at the Holiday Inn Beach Resort in Montego Bay. He was still married to Marva, and they had two wonderful girls, Samantha and Sue Helen. Unfortunately, Karl was unable to forgive his mother for leaving him with his dad while the rest of the family flourished in Montego Bay.

He hated Essie for all of her shortcomings as a single mother, and he was vocal about it. Essie loved him anyway and tried many times to ask for his forgiveness, but Karl could not find it in his heart to forgive her.

Karl was an honest and upright Christian in the Glenworth SDA Church, and it was because of his honesty and truthfulness that he could not hide his feelings. He loved God. He loved his kids. He loved his father. He loved all mankind, but he hated Essie.

He hated his mother like a rat hated a dose of poison. It hurt him deeply inside every time he thought about the life he had in the country as a boy growing up with his father, Tim. No one ever knew his full story because he never said much about why he so despised his time in the country. They just assumed that a country life spoke for itself.

Karl did not attend his parents' wedding, and he never accepted Essie's offer to file for him to migrate to the United States with his siblings. He turned down the offer. She sent him the immigration form anyway, for him to sign so that he and his kids could all travel together, but he tore it to pieces. He refused to take anything from his mother. He often called her a "dirty whore." He did not care for his mother to file for him. Moreover, he got himself a ten-year U.S. visitor visa so he could travel whenever he wanted. For the time being, he wanted to stay in Jamaica and take care of his family, because after all, he had a great job at a large, popular hotel. Nevertheless, Karl, many years later, traveled on his own to Florida and then to New York to live temporarily.

When Essie was not at home in New York with Gena and Myrtle, she enjoyed visiting other nearby states like New Jersey and Connecticut where other family members, such as her cousins Jenifer and Junior, who were brother and sister, lived.

It was clear that Essie was having the time of her life as an honorable New York City resident, the ultimate big city. However, she never forgot her striving family, which was dispersed all over the globe.

Chapter 31

At seventy-six years old, Essie, the naive country girl from Cascade, was relished the peak of her life in New York. To say that she was enjoying herself would be a true understatement.

She was as happy as a frolicking, zealous New Yorker at the Labor Day Parade in Brooklyn, or at the Macy's Thanksgiving Day Parade in Manhattan.

She never let anything get her down. She shook off any problems that came her way with the use of a prayer or two. She got a kick out of living high on life. She became very compliant with her health care and medications. She made no more dull, balky, unenthusiastic comments about living. She was luxuriating in the esteem and enjoyment of her grandkids and great-grandkids. She wanted to live forever.

However, Essie knew better. She knew that we all have to relinquish life at some point. We can hope for a long, happy, productive life, but sooner or later, we all must abate. She fought her ailments aggressively.

She was diagnosed with diabetes, Parkinson's disease, rheumatoid arthritis, osteoarthritis, generalized hypertension, heart disease, glaucoma, peripheral neuralgia—specifically, peripheral neuropathy—and two mild, silent heart attacks.

Although Essie wanted to live forever, she began having a strange feeling that the end was near, as her health was rapidly and acutely declining. She decided that when she died, she would like for it to happen while she was in her own home in Glenworth, Jamaica. She called Gena and said, "My dear child, I want to go home to expire in my rocking chair on my veranda in Glenworth."

"But, Mom, do you remember that you lost your passport book and all of your traveling documents on your last trip to Jamaica? Do you remember that you had a difficult time coming back? We'll have to take care of those things at the immigration office downtown, so you can travel again."

"Okay then, please try and get them for me. Please hurry, because I'm not feeling too good in my body, and I want to go home to Jamaica."

"Why do you have to go to Jamaica? What's wrong with being right here in New York? There's no one there to help you as much as here, and remember, Mom, health care is not that great there."

"Well, Gena, I don't care. I want to die in my home that I worked so hard for."

Gena got busy trying to regain her mother's travel documents, but one year later, the processing was still unfinished. Essie pleaded with Gena to try harder with the U.S. Embassy to see if they could speed up the process.

Essie became anxious and irritated because she wanted to go home at any cost. She was tired of waiting. The one year that she had waited on her travel documents could have been spent in her home in Glenworth.

Unfortunately, Essie, the orphan child, the city girl, the single mother, the religious fanatic wife, did not make it home to Glenworth. She had a stroke at the age of seventy-seven. This stroke left her partially paralyzed in New York hospital.

After three weeks of unsuccessful medical intervention, she had a second, disastrous stroke that left her totally paralyzed and unable to speak. Although she was in a fragile situation, she resisted the hands of death for almost one and a half years.

Maybe she held on for her travel documents to successfully process processed, so that she could go home to Jamaica and depart in a peaceful manner in her home in Glenworth.

Essie's home in Glenworth was clearly either the breaking point in her life, or the breakthrough point in her life. Whichever it was, it defined her life.

Essie spent her remaining time in a popular nursing home in New York City.

She reflected on whole life, including her successes and failures. She had succeeded in giving her kids an average life. She had succeeded in finding a good man to be her husband. She had succeeded in making it in a rough city like Montego Bay. But she had failed in giving her kids the best life that they could have. She had failed in giving her kids a father early in their lives when they needed one most. She had failed to make it big-time in Montego Bay.

The grim reality was that she had failed in all of the same areas that she had succeeded. On the other hand, the truth was that she had succeeded in all of the areas where she had failed.

Essie thought about her mother. She thought about what her life would have been like, or could have been like, growing up with Doris Lynn, the mother that she never met. She often wondered why God took her at such a young age. Her mother never had the chance to see her face. She wondered if her mother had been alive, would she have been proud of the way she had lived her life.

She thought about the father she never met. She thought about the man who raped her mother and produced an orphan child. Yes, the perverse fact was that her father had raped her mother. That was the big secret that her mother Doris Lynn, died with. That was the reason her mother refused to discuss any information about the mysterious father of her expected child. Doris Lynn was ashamed and embarrassed because she had been violated by her first cousin.

Doris Lynn was violated at the back of a church by one of her visiting cousins from Kingston by the name of Lester Brown. Essie, by chance, found out about it from Miriam, her cousin in Mt. Salem.

The problem was that she was told about it long after Lester Brown had died in a car accident. Miriam confessed to Essie that it was due to the pure sorrow, guilt, and pity that she felt within her that she was compelled to help her with her baby, Lela. Lela was born around the same time Miriam first found out about the rape. Miriam asked Essie to keep it a secret to protect the integrity of the family.

Essie had nothing but undisturbed time also to reflect on her kids, who had broken through thick, seemingly impenetrable barriers to get to where they were going. Gena, for instance, had made a simple promise to go and prepare a place for the family in the United States, and she did so like a soldier bushwhacking her way against all odds.

She also had time to reflect on how Leonard, at age ten, had envisioned himself being a doctor. She wondered how he was able to fight his way to the top in such an amazing way to become a doctor.

She couldn't have been happier, although he was not a physician as promised. She was still proud of him because he had delivered to her the status of a doctor, and that was more than what she, a plain, simple, naive country girl, could have asked for from one of the seeds that she had planted on this earth.

She thought of how proud she was when she attended his graduation at Nova Southeastern University in Florida. That was one of her proudest moments by far. She remembered Leonard also promised to write a book about her life before she died.

She remembered sitting down and spilling her guts while he videotaped her. He meticulously videotaped her for hours on one of her vacations at his home in Florida as she spoke about the ups and downs in her life. She thought that it would have been good to see that accomplishment so she could check it off her "bucket list," but she was proud of him anyway.

Essie reflected on the lawsuit she won against the Catholic church across the street from her building in New York City. She fell in front of the church gate one day while crossing their driveway and sprained her ankles. She was unable to walk for months. She was encouraged to file a lawsuit against the church.

She won ten thousand dollars. After winning that grand sum, she remembered her promise to put a second level on her home in Glenworth. That was what she did with the award from the court. She sent it to Bunny in Jamaica to do the construction on her home. Essie wondered with guilt if she had done the right thing by suing the church. Was that why the house in Glenworth stood as an incomplete monument of her desire? She knew that if there was a crossroad in her life, it was when she had to choose, for or against, obtaining a permanent roof over her kids' heads.

Chapter 32

Junior had been one of the first direct beneficiaries of the family's house in Glenworth. He alone did not benefited from the house; the whole family benefited when they moved into their new home, but Junior was the first to benefit from the land. When he had his first daughter, Denise, with Pauline, the runaway teen, they moved out of the house and built a cozy two-bedroom house in the backyard of Essie's property.

This meant that he did not have to buy land to build his house. He did not have to pay any related fees, such as taxes. The only permission he needed was Essie's, and she was happy to see the young couple blossom into a loving, independent family with a home of their own.

Junior and Pauline had two more kids after Denise migrated to the United States, a girl named Paula and a boy named Caple. The name Caple derived from the name of a famous reggae singer called Capleton. The singer was famous for coining the phrase, "Fire a go bun them."

Junior and his family enjoyed a peaceful life in Essie's backyard. Pauline hustled as a local vender for tourists and local citizens. Junior increased his clientele as he marketed his skill as an electrician. No one interfered with them, but unfortunately, they were their own worst enemies. There were times when they would have a serious argument that escalated into a fist fight. Yes, there was domestic abuse. However, don't feel too sorry for Pauline. While it was Junior who usually started the arguments it was Pauline who was the first and only one throwing the punches. Junior just duck or dodge Pauline's punches.

He never threw a punch at Pauline. He tried to contain her by holding her two hands as long as he could to try to stop her. What was amazing was that when the fight was over, Pauline cried the loudest. Junior victoriously walked away with a swollen face or black eye.

Everyone automatically ran to Pauline's rescue because she was crying so hard. No one understood that Pauline was crying because she could not get as many punches in as she would have liked. It was always the same story. Junior, in principle, didn't believe in hitting a female because Essie had taught him well, But he was the jealous guy who started the argument and ended up being physically abused.

He was also the person who wrongfully was screamed at by everyone. Pauline, on the other hand, had a sharp temper like Mike Tyson and a right hand like Mohammed Ali. She was opinionated and did not take kindly to anyone telling her what to do. She, by nature, enjoyed a good fight.

With her hostile attitude, it was good riddance for Junior when his mother filed for him and his children to migrate to the United States. Not knowing that Junior was on the verge of getting his immigration approval, Pauline moved out of Junior's house two months before he traveled to the United States. She moved out to go and live with another man. This man did well in Jamaica and did better than Junior. He had a big, fancy house and a lot of money.

Pauline had found the man that she had been looking for the day she ran away from her parents in May Pen. The only problem was that she now had three kids and was much older. However, the kids were not a problem for her. She left them all in Junior's care. One day, she packed her bags and left Junior and all her kids behind.

Thank goodness for Junior, Essie's filing process was right on time. Junior migrated to Florida, where he lived with Leonard and his family for one month. He thought that Florida was too slow for him in terms of job opportunities, so he moved on to New York City. He left Paula behind to stay at his house in Jamaica to watch over it while she took care of some health issues.

Unfortunately, Caple died shortly after his migration to New York at the tender age of twelve from a grand mal epileptic seizure.

Even after her health issues were cleared up, Paula, refused to travel. Instead, she decided to stay and enjoy the peace of mind she got by living on her own in the family home

***

Betty's story was different from Junior's. She was independent and easygoing. As long as her beauty parlor was open for business and clients were available, she was happy. She placed all of her time and effort into her business, but with little financial return.

244

Although she was good at the art of hairdressing, she was awful as a businesswoman. She was too kindhearted to recoup a profit from her business. She gave away more free services to her clients than the Salvation Army gave away in a lifetime. She made many attempts to move out of Essie's house in Glenworth, but when business was rough or her relationship was bad, she moved right back in with her mother. She had her first kids, twins, in Essie's house.

She also had her other children in that home. She had six kids altogether, and they all stayed with their grandmother, Essie, while Betty worked day and night in her salon. The most significant point in Betty's life came when Essie migrated to the United States and filed for her and all six of her kids. They went to live in Essie's apartment in New York City.

Betty was not happy in New York, so she decided to leave her kids with their grandmother and return to Jamaica to attend to her business. Betty moved back in the house in Glenworth where Bunny lived with his wife and kids. Bunny was not happy to share the house with Betty. Betty and he were cut from two different cloths. Betty was not ambitious or domesticated around the house when it came to chores, while Bunny and his family were ambitious, tidy, and well organized. They could not get along. Bunny moved his family out and left the house to Betty. Betty lived happily in the house for the rest of her life, which, unfortunately, was not long.

Betty met a boyfriend, Kenneth, who was initially good to her. He bought a new refrigerator, a stove, and some furniture for the house where they both lived happily. Betty was in love with him

He and Betty lived a good life together until they broke up one day. Kenneth decided to leave Betty and find a place of his own.

This was an unpleasant surprise to Betty. Kenneth moved all of the new, fancy kitchen accoutrements and furniture out of the house He moved about one block away with a new girlfriend.

Betty could not deal with the shocking breakup. Distressed, she started experiencing significant weight loss due to excess worry and depression.

Within six months, she had two brain aneurisms that ruptured in her head. Medical staff tried to save her at the hospital, but she died.

After Betty's untimely death at age forty-nine, the house was left to Lance, Betty's youngest son, and Dean, Myrtle's only son. Lance moved out of the house and put his room up for rent.

Dean was the only family member who remained in the house. It is ironic that the sole son of Myrtle was inheriting Essie's house.

Essie's house did not have any effect on Lela. Lela grew up with her cousin Miriam. Therefore, Lela had no true dealings with the house. The only time Lela came in contact with the house was when she popped into Glenworth to see how her biological family was doing.

***

Karl, on the other hand, benefited from living at Essie's house. He moved from the country when he was fourteen years old. However, before had moved in with his mother, Karl visited his family in the city at least once or twice per year.

Karl had the ability to catch on to the latest fashions or behaviors. The family looked forward to his visits from the country. It was fun to see the new styles that were arising. One time, he came to visit the family with a new style of walking that the family called "the country walk." When he walked, he used one foot to hit the heel of the other foot, creating a dance-like walking or hopping motion.

The following visit, he walked normally, but then the latest style was to suck on his inner bicep with his arm thrown across his shoulder while walking. This action created a look as if he was hiding his face with one of his hands across his mouth and resting on his shoulder.

On another visit, Karl combined the two styles, the foot hitting and the bicep sucking, as he walked. It was a pleasure, mostly for the younger kids, to see him display the latest styles from the country when he came to visit.

At age fourteen, Karl brought his few belongings to move in with his family. He demanded that he had the right to live with his family in Glenworth.

He spent his teenage years with his family in the city. He joined the Glenworth SDA church where he fortuitously discovered a new talent he didn't know he had. He was an excellent singer. He and his two friends, Rodney and Paul, started a male singing group. They became so popular that they visited different churches to perform concerts.

Karl met his wife, Marva, at the Glenworth SDA church. She was a teacher. They got married and moved out of Essie's house and built a nice, three-bedroom house in a newly developed district of Rose Hall called The Little Spot.

They had two wonderful girls, Samantha and Sue Helen. Samantha grew up to be a teacher like her mother and Sue Helen wanted to attend medical school to become a doctor, like her Uncle Leonard.

Karl's resentment toward his mother grew stronger over time. Although he was a great person and a wonderful Christian, he showed open resentment to Essie for leaving him behind in the country with his father. However, Karl did not deny the fact that Essie's house was a refuge for him as it allowed him to escape the country at an early age so he could redeem himself as a valuable member of the big-city society.

Next to Lela, the house in Glenworth had the least effect on Leonard. Other than it allowed him to dream big dreams and aspire for greatness, Leonard spent the least amount of time in the house. He was one of the first family members that Gena brought to the United States. Leonard left Essie's house at the age of sixteen to live with Gena in New York City. Decades later, almost ten years after the death of his mother, he was able to fulfill his delayed promise to pen a book about her and her house in Glenworth.

***

Essie's house in Glenworth was a motivating factor in Bunny's life. The greatest benefit started taking root in Bunny's life when his family migrated to the United States, leaving him and his wife and two kids in Jamaica.

Prior to that time, Bunny had been getting his life together. With him being Essie's youngest child, he felt that he had a lot of time on his hands. However, that was only until he met Joyce. Joyce became a strong motivating force in Bunny's life. He started going to the library in downtown Montego Bay to do research on leather crafts. He also started developing a strong interest in local politics. One day, he made a call to Leonard asking for his insight on his new leather project.

"Hey there, brother. How are you and the family doing this wonderful day that the good Lord has made for us?" Bunny asked.

"I'm doing well, my brother. My wife and my stepson are doing great also. I can't complain. As you have said, He gave us life and this wonderful day, one can't complain much. Thanks for asking. How are things going with you in Jamaica?"

"Well, I met a nice girl named Joyce. She is really a go-getter, and we are looking for ways to start our future together. She does buying and selling in the local tourist market, and I'm doing some self-educating in the library. I'm looking into the leather craft business. I noticed that there are lots of crafts in Jamaica, but few utilize the raw material of the cows here. I want to start from the basic raw material and build a strong chain network as a foundation of my business."

"That sounds great, bro. I'm proud of you. You are taking a stand to strengthen your future. I like your idea. It sounds like you got yourself a niche market. But you know, you have to jump on it fast before it gets cold."

"No, mon, this idea cannot get cold. I'd this fire burning inside of me for a while now, and I'm trying to see how I can get started. There are some things that I'm going to need to get started. I need the proper tools and a few other things. I'm taking things step-by-step."

"Hey, tell you what, bro. I'll look around and see what I can find over here in Florida. As soon as I find something, I'll give you a buzz."

"Hey, brother, you read my mind. Thank you, my brother. May the good Lord bless you and your family. Say hello to her for me."

"I will. Bye for now. Love you, bro."

"Love you too, brother. Bye."

Within two weeks, Leonard located a leather shop. He purchased a starter kit with all the necessary tools needed to do leather crafting. He sent it to Bunny, which started his leather business.

Bunny never looked back. His business grew stronger and more profitable each day. The gift that Leonard sent him, even with its small price tag, was worth more than a million dollars.

Having a growing business in Jamaica and his wife's growing business endeavors, he started having a family of his own. They had two lovely boys and a little princess girl. They also adopted another charming girl into their family unit. They flourished in Jamaica. They lived in Essie's house. Bunny's family was proud of their home, so they kept it clean and neat. They also made improvements to the house to make it look more presentable. They were truly comfortable. They benefited directly from Essie's house in Glenworth.

The benefit of living in Essie's house started dwindling when Betty returned to Jamaica. Bunny and his family were disappointed because they never thought that they would have to share the house with anyone, let alone someone who had migrated to the United States.

Moreover, Betty was not domestic and did not care to make the same effort of keeping up the house. A rivalry brewed between the two parties, which escalated into an outright verbal fight between the two siblings.

It was time to call in the big chief, Mrs. Essie Brown. She was notified of the rising animosity over issues concerning rights and means for a peaceful coexistence in the house.

Essie packed her bag and headed to Jamaica to settle the fuss. Once Essie arrived, the fire escalated. Being a strong advocate for female rights and safety, was partial in dealing with the issues. Essie believed that Bunny, being a man, should be the one to leave the house if he could not live peacefully with Betty.

Anger became a brutal force. Bunny blazed up in a fury. He was angry with his mother. However, Bunny found the respectable chivalry deep within him to compose himself as he calmly brought his mother outside and pointed to a fancy, two-story house across the street. He said, "Do you see that house, Mother? Take a good look at it. I, Bunny Dun, I am going to build myself that same house. Believe me. I don't need to live in your house. Mother, listen to me and listen well. You and Betty can go to you know where' in this house. I don't care to live here anymore." Bunny's eyes were as red as fire. He could not hold back his anger any longer.

That same day, he condemned his mother's house and moved his belongings out to go and live with his wife's mother in a simple, worn-out, two-bedroom house.

However, the conflict with Essie and Betty lit a fire within Bunny that never died. He was motivated to find a spot and build a house exactly like his old neighbor's house

This was the driving force for Bunny and his wife to resurge back to the top. They took their game plan to another level. Joyce started traveling abroad where she would buy clothes and other items at a low retail cost and return to Jamaica to resell them for a large profit.

Bunny also stepped up his game as he started working longer hours and making stronger social and political network connections. In a short time, they found a piece of land on which to build their dream home.

It was a beautiful spot on a hill that overlooked the Montego Bay, Sangster's International Airport, and the picturesque ocean. They built their home starting from a modest, two-bedroom, basic structure. Over the years, they added to it, one room at a time, until it started taking shape.

It was a true duplicate of Essie's neighbor's house, as Bunny had so confidently promised.

When Essie won the lawsuit against the Catholic church, she sent the ten thousand dollars of award money in two portions to Bunny for him to use to complete her dream of adding a second level to her house in Glenworth.

For the life of her, Essie could not imagine the depth of built-up emotions that her beloved "wash belly" was holding against her. She thought she had done the right thing, so it was difficult for her to see that her son would not forgive her for taking sides with her daughter.

Bunny knew in his heart, just like Karl, that he could not forgive his mother, but he took the job and the money to do the job.

He did the best he could do with the funds, but Essie's house was not completed as expected. Bunny reported that the money ran out because most of it was paid on labor. Essie was disappointed, but she was happy to see the improvements to Bunny's home on top of the hill on the other side of Glenworth District.

Years passed and things began to seem normal. Betty was enjoying Essie's modest and incomplete house in Glenworth, and Bunny and his family were enjoying their fancy, two-story dream home. Betty and Bunny became cordial and polite to each other.

However, the grudge, bitterness, and anger ran deep within Bunny's veins. The bitterness could be seen at the graveside at Essie's funeral after her body was shipped to Jamaica for her second funeral service and burial.

Bunny and his wife were put in charge of the funeral preparations and related activities. They

253

both did an excellent job as far as the preparation of the funeral was concerned. After all, it was Bunny's mother, and he could not afford to give her anything less than what society at Glenworth expected.

Although the show must go on, Bunny was only human so, like Karl, who walked up to his mother's casket to condemn her, Bunny also walked up to his mother's grave when the funeral service was over. He stood still for a moment. He reflected on that day when his mother took sides with his sister against him. He panted heavily. His body was tense and his heart pounded like the beat of a drum. The rage boiled up in him all over again and he was hit hard with a savage blow of anger. He stood on his mother's grave and said:

—Mother, it was hard, very hard, hard as could ever be. But I forgive you. When I was twelve, you taught me how to forgive.

THE END

Made in the USA
Charleston, SC
15 March 2013